PENGUIN BOOKS
MELUSINE

Silent and brooding, the cr⋯ ⋯
remote French countrysi⋯ ⋯
as a holiday house to Rog⋯ ⋯
nor his sisters – to break the ⋯ ⋯ ⋯er
holidays by the sea in Pem⋯ ⋯ ⋯ertainly
Chateau de Bois Serpe wasn⋯ ⋯ ⋯hat the travel
agent had described. Roger's pa⋯nts were horrified by
its run-down condition; but it wasn't just the dirt and
decay – nor even the obvious decades of neglect. There
was an underlying strangeness about the Chateau de
Bois Serpe and its owners: sullen, unkempt Monsieur
Serpe, and his daughter Melusine, with her expression-
less black eyes.

So why did Roger feel so strongly drawn to her? What
was it that attracted him to an elusive girl who spent her
days tending her father's goats – a girl who didn't even
speak his language? Pity mixed with fascination was a
part of it; but as their friendship developed, so did
Roger's awareness of the mystery surrounding Melusine.
Only he could interpret the true meaning behind her cry
for help – what he could not know was that in responding
to it he would involve himself and his family in
undreamed-of consequences . . .

Lynne Reid Banks was born in London and was evacu-
ated to Canada during the war. On her return to
England she became an actress, and then wrote plays
for the theatre, radio and television. She worked in
television, and then emigrated to Israel, where she mar-
ried a sculptor. They lived on a kibbutz for nine years
and have three sons. She now lives with her husband in
Dorset.

MELUSINE

A MYSTERY

by

LYNNE REID BANKS

PENGUIN BOOKS

PENGUIN BOOKS

Published by the Penguin Group
27 Wrights Lane, London W8 5TZ, England
Viking Penguin Inc., 40 West 23rd Street, New York, New York 10010, USA
Penguin Books Australia Ltd, Ringwood, Victoria, Australia
Penguin Books Canada Ltd, 2801 John Street, Markham, Ontario, Canada L3R 1B4
Penguin Books (NZ) Ltd, 182–190 Wairau Road, Auckland 10, New Zealand

Penguin Books Ltd, Registered Offices: Harmondsworth, Middlesex, England

First published by Hamish Hamilton's Children's Books, 1988
Published in Penguin Books 1990
1 3 5 7 9 10 8 6 4 2

Printed and bound in Great Britain by
Cox & Wyman Ltd, Reading
Filmset in Baskerville

27021195

To Joan Benham
For all the ups and downs

Contents

1   The Journey

Roger sat between his twin sisters in the back of the family car and stared across each of their necks in turn at the countryside flashing by.

The twins were grizzling and sniping at each other without cease, and had been ever since they'd left Paris that morning. They'd liked Paris; they'd have been quite happy to stay there for the whole holiday. They'd gone mad about the little street cafés with their *citrons pressés*; they'd put away *crêpes* till they'd looked like them; they'd gawped at the passers-by and giggled and pointed till even their mother lost patience. The twins had been furious when their parents had said there wasn't time to go up the Eiffel Tower if they were going to make it to the chateau by nightfall. And they'd been griping ever since, making Roger's life a misery.

What a huge country France was, thought Roger as they drove mile after mile and hour after hour. He was getting sick of being squashed between those two boring, boring girls. Would they never shut up and let him look through the window in peace?

'Can't I sit on the outside?' he begged several times, when he could get a word in.

'I'm sorry, darling,' said his mother from the passenger seat in front. 'You must sit between the girls and keep them apart – if they start hitting each other, Dad'll go mad.'

Roger sighed heavily and wriggled back a bit so that he was slightly behind them and not right between. They were leaning forward to squabble across him, so he was able to look out of the nearside window behind Emma's neck, almost an unobstructed view for once. The fields of sweet corn swept past like an army with lances, alternating with smiling yellow acres of big-faced sunflowers; the only break in the pleasant monotony was an occasional village or isolated farmhouse.

Suddenly Roger sat up straight and turned, ricking his neck. He twisted and scrambled till he could kneel up and look behind, through the rear window.

'Oh, sit still, can't you?' peeved Polly. 'Keep your dirty shoes off my skirt. Ow! Mum, he's kicking!'

'Sit round properly, Roger,' ordered their father. He was getting tired. 'We'll be there in half an hour.'

Roger sat round, reluctantly. He was frowning. Had he really seen what he thought he'd seen? After a few minutes he saw it again.

'Look!'

He pointed, but by the time the others had turned their heads they'd gone past.

'What?' the twins asked.

'A huge question mark!'

'What are you on about?'

'I saw a big question mark on that barn we passed. I saw one just now as well. It was – like – painted on. Huge.'

'You're round the twist,' said Polly contemptuously.

'Did you see it, Dad?'

'I've got to watch the road, and it's damn well putting me to sleep,' said his father.

'Let me drive for a bit,' said their mother.

The twins groaned loudly. It was their contention that their kind, gentle mother turned into a maniac as soon as she got behind the wheel. Their father, who privately agreed with them, sat up hastily and opened the window.

'We're nearly there now!' he said briskly, sounding very awake.

They weren't.

By the time they actually arrived it was pitch dark, but

8

before that Roger had seen two more of the question marks. He didn't say any more about them, but gazed at them until the car had left them behind. They filled the whole end wall of buildings. He had no idea what they were for. They gave him a funny feeling – as if there were a question mark over the whole area they were going to. Or over the holiday.

The chateau stood up against the stars, a great spooky shape with a wide round tower at one end which stuck up above the straight line of the roof. The car bumped over long grass and ruts. There was no road, and no lights at all except the car headlights. It was a wonder they'd managed to find it, and Emma sounded as if she wished they hadn't when she said, 'Ugh, what a horrible black-looking place!' Polly was asleep.

They got out stiffly. There was a strong animal smell in the air, and the lonely sound of frogs and crickets. Their father took a torch and played it over the building.

'We must have missed the drive somehow,' he muttered. 'This seems to be the back. What a weird place – it looks deserted.'

'It's very overgrown,' said their mother. 'And ramshackle! Look at those shutters, they're half hanging off.'

'I do think they might have left a light on,' said their father. 'I mean, they do know we're coming, don't they?'

Emma had shaken Polly awake. She stumbled out of the car and at once gave a little shriek.

'Ugh! I think I've trodden in some cow-muck!'

Their mother had located a door and was now banging on it.

'Hallo!' she called, in her very English voice. '*Nous sommes arrivés!*'

After a few moments they heard noises, and then the door creaked open. A man of about forty, with a thin, grizzled face and rough clothes, appeared in the torch's beam. He had a torch of his own and shone it back at them, first on one and then another till he'd seen them all. There was an awkward pause. Then he said gruffly, '*Bonjour. Entrez.*' And stood aside to let them in.

They walked in single file into a dimly-lit, stone-walled corridor and huddled there until the man had bolted the door after them and gone ahead into a room at the end. They followed him, the girls nudging and stifling nervous giggles, while their mother hissed: 'Behave yourselves now!'

The room they found themselves in was a huge, cavernous, incredibly old-fashioned kitchen. It reminded Roger of the one in 'Jack and the Beanstalk', presided over by the ogre. It was lit by a single oil lamp, and the glowing remains of a fire. The fireplace was almost as big as a small room. Huge logs had been burning; now only their ends were left, with a few smouldering embers between them.

In front of this was a very long, narrow table, covered with oil-cloth, over which the lamp was hanging. There were a great many things on the table including pots, pans, plates, a wine bottle, newspapers, tools and all sorts of rubbish. It looked as if the man had been eating his dinner out of a huge old iron frying-pan with a long handle. There was a chunk of French bread sticking out of a mess of fried egg.

As Roger, who was extremely hungry, edged irresistibly closer to the food, something happened to the table. There had been black patches on the oil-cloth which he had taken for stains. But as he came closer the patches suddenly came alive, moved as one, and rose up with sullen buzzing. Roger's mother let out a gasp.

'They're flies!' she whispered.

'*Avez-vous faim?*' the man asked shortly.

In halting French, Roger's father said that perhaps some bread and butter for the children. . . . Soon they were all seated at the fly-blown table, trying to keep their elbows and hands out of the patches of grease and the puddles of wine while the Frenchman hacked lengths off a long loaf and pushed blackened knives and a packet of well-excavated butter towards them. He then filled three glasses with wine

10

for the children ('Ugh! I'm not drinking *this!*' muttered Emma, but Roger tossed his down without even tasting it, he was so thirsty) and two small glasses of some other drink for their parents.

Roger's father drank some, and choked. 'Wow!' he exclaimed. '*C'est très fort, ça. Très bon!*' He held out his glass for more.

'*Vous demeurez ici seul?*' asked his mother politely.

'*J'ai une petite fille,*' the man grunted.

'Only one?' asked Roger's mother, rather waggishly due to nervousness. The man looked blank. '*Er – vous avez – seulement – une enfant?*' She held up one finger.

The man said in an angry voice, '*J'en ai deux. L'autre fille n'habite pas chez moi.*' Roger thought what a bad-tempered man he seemed, and wondered why he advertised for guests if every simple question annoyed him.

Roger's father interrupted firmly. 'I think it's time we got to bed.' He stood up. 'Could we see the – er – our part of the — ?'

'If our part is anything like this,' Emma whispered to Polly, 'I'll *die.*' She hadn't eaten a thing, and had sat well back from the table with a look of disgust on her face. Roger, while not relishing the flies or the wine-puddles, thought the huge old kitchen was exciting. Especially the great fireplace and all the shadowy nooks and crannies in the stone walls. It really was like something out of a book, and he looked forward to seeing it by daylight, and exploring the rest of the chateau as well.

Meanwhile the owner, whose name was Monsieur Serpe, led the way to a door in a far, dark corner. He fitted a large iron key, like a jailer's, into an enormous square lock and turned it with a grinding noise. Then he switched on a light on the other side.

The girls, crowding through under their father's arm, gasped in amazement. The difference was incredible – the contrast between the gloomy, grimy kitchen behind them,

11

and this! Even their mother could not restrain a little murmur of delighted relief.

A large, beautifully furnished room opened out before them. The switch had illuminated an elegant ceiling light-fitting like a brass octopus with a pointed bulb in each tentacle. The walls were hung with paintings and tapestries, except one, which was lined with beautiful old books. The chairs were covered with brocade, and there was an eight-sided table in the middle which looked like something in a museum – it was inlaid with coloured stone in a magnificent polished pattern.

The others seemed absolutely enchanted with all this, and ran about touching things and exclaiming in wonder at the grandeur of it all. Roger, for his part, felt rather daunted. It wasn't the sort of room he could ever be comfortable in – he'd be worried the whole time that he might damage something.

But there must be other rooms. He found a door and went through it. On the other side was another superb room with a double bed in it – not a four-poster, but still very grand. Beyond that was another bedroom. This one had two little beds, each on a raised tiled platform-thing with steps leading up and a wrought-iron railing around them, as if each bed stood on its own little balcony. The rest of the room was on a lower level, the sunken floor covered with a gorgeous thick red and blue rug.

Roger sighed. He knew who would sleep here, and it wouldn't be him. *His* room, which he found leading off the kitchen, was the smallest in the place – it looked as if it had once been a walk-in larder. He groped for the light-switch to inspect it, and as he did so he froze.

There was someone else in the room. Someone – or something.

His eye had been caught by a brief movement on the floor near the bed. The only light, which came from behind him, stretched its rectangle across the floor, stopping just short of the bed which could hardly be seen. But something had flickered, or shifted somehow, just near the bed leg.

Was some intruder hiding there?

Roger's hand on the switch unfroze, but he didn't turn the light on. What had that police officer said when he'd visited the school? 'Never tackle a burglar, he might go for you. Leave his exit clear. . . .' At the time, Roger had thought that was idiotic. What, let a thief escape? But suddenly he understood. He turned and ran back into the first big room.

'Mum! Dad! I think there's someone under my bed!'

Every face in the room turned to him. He had time to notice Monsieur Serpe's especially. It had gone deathly white beneath the short grizzled hair and stubbly beard. While the others were pelting Roger with questions and his father was brushing past him to go and investigate, Monsieur Serpe seemed to vanish – he just melted backwards through the connecting door into his own dismal abode, and Roger heard the big key turn.

The twins were for once giving Roger all their attention.

'Did you actually *see* him?'

'Where?'

'What did he look like?'

Before he could draw breath to answer, though, his father called, and they all trooped through. The light was now on in the cupboard-bedroom off the kitchen. It was not only the smallest but certainly the plainest room in the apartment, with nothing grand or interesting about it at all. It really was like a larder, or perhaps a monk's cell, with a low ceiling and whitewashed walls and a flag floor. No rug, let alone a gorgeous one. The little bed was like an army cot. There wasn't even a proper window, just a tiny dark hole with rusty netting stretched over it. Shelves, a straight chair . . . that was all. And absolutely no intruder to be seen.

Of course they all laughed at him (except his mother, who was exploring the kitchen).

'Trust old Rodge to dream up a burglar!'

'It must've been that wine he was swigging!'

'I'm not so sure it was a person,' said Roger defensively. 'I just saw something move. It might have been a rat.'

The girls burst into mock shrieks. His father went out of the room – which was crowded with four of them in it – giving him a friendly cuff on the behind.

'Go to bed, the lot of you,' called their mother. 'The holiday starts tomorrow.'

2   *Goat Girl*

Roger woke up very early, despite his late night. A ray of
sunlight pierced the screen on his little round window
and touched his face with a dusty finger. He sat up in the
narrow bed and put his feet on to the cold stone flags.

His small room by daylight (not that much got in) didn't
displease him. It was clean and simple. There were some
shelves left over from its larder days, and he lost no time in
unpacking and arranging on these his sketchpad, *Mad* maga-
zine, current book of ghost stories, lucky owl that went with
him everywhere, and his clock radio, except there was
nowhere to plug it in, which was rather irritating. His clothes
he left in a jumble in his case. Then he pulled on some shorts,
sandals and a T-shirt and went out of the room.

Their kitchen – as clean and modern as the other one had
been old-fashioned and filthy – was flooded with sunlight. It
was also absolutely abuzz with flies. Except last night in the
other kitchen, Roger had never seen so many – they were all
over everything. He quickly closed the door to his room to
keep them out – there hadn't been one in there, due to the
screen window, and he meant to keep it that way.

His mother had brought a cardboard box of groceries to
tide them over till they could get to the local village shops.
He helped himself to some Ryvita and peanut butter, and
slipped out of the back door into the French morning.

The air smelt entirely different from at home. The animal
smell was very strong now. It was like a cow-smell, but not
quite. Under that dominating one, there were others – faint,

vagrant scents which he couldn't identify. They must come from flowers unknown in England, or perhaps it was just something in the air. The grass and trees looked just the same. . . . An area of rough grass which had obviously never seen a lawnmower stretched away from the back step to a broken stone wall. Beyond was countryside, empty of people and infinitely alluring. Roger hurled himself into a fast, exuberant run at the broken area of the wall, and leapt over it.

He found himself in a rutted lane overhung by tall trees. He followed it to the right, keeping parallel with the chateau which was on the other side of the wall. The chateau really was enormous. Its squat round tower, with its turret and weathercock, was the tallest part – it was three storeys high to the chateau's two. The rest took the form of an E without its middle prong, and there was a second tower at the other angle, but this was in ruins.

It took Roger four minutes by his digital watch to walk to a turning in the lane, indicating the size of the building.

'There must be other people living there,' he thought. 'How could just Monsieur Serpe and his daughter, and summer visitors, live in all that?'

More walking brought him round to the back. Suddenly the stable smell was stronger than ever, making him want to hold his nose. He heard an outburst of country noise – a mass bleating. Sheep? He began to run.

A break in the wall, which had once contained a tall gate now corroding off its hinges, led him to a corner of the chateau. Built carelessly against the high stone wall was a large shelter, open on two sides. It was just stout wooden props with a corrugated-iron roof. Around it was a fence. Inside, it was floored with thick straw. And scattered everywhere, bleating and capering, were dozens of goats.

Roger stopped short, staring. He had seen the odd goat before – usually large, rather fierce-looking creatures, tethered in fields or behind a traveller's caravan. These were small and appealing, mostly brown and white, with soft floppy ears and little beards and inquisitive, bony faces. Their small scuts wagged cheerily as they wandered or jumped about. Most of them had horns. And all of them had udders.

Roger might not have noticed the udders except that someone was in the midst of the herd, very busy getting milk out of them.

She was a girl of about his own age, or a bit older. He couldn't see anything except her back, at first. She had long black hair pulled into a pigtail. She wore filthy jeans and a green T-shirt with a diamond pattern on it. She sat on a tiny three-legged stool, bent with her head against a goat's flank. Through the bird-song, fly-buzzing and bleating, Roger could hear the steady dring-dring, dring-dring of the streams of milk hitting the tin pail.

When she'd finished that goat, she stood up, picked up the pail and the stool, and moving over to another, grabbed it fearlessly by the horns, and dragged it to where she wanted it. With astonishing nimbleness she kicked the stool into position and sat on it, drew the pail into place with one hand, and proceeded to milk the goat. Roger, lurking in the shadows, timed her – four and a half minutes. Then she let the goat go, and carried the pail through a doorway into the darkness of a corner of the chateau.

He waited.

When she came out again, having emptied the pail, she saw him standing at the fence. She stopped dead for a moment. Then, without a flicker of a smile, she walked on. This time the goat she wanted frisked its head and began to move away as soon as she began to milk it. The girl tried to grab one of its horns and accidentally kicked the pail over. Luckily there wasn't much in it.

'*Merde!*' she exclaimed furiously.

Roger, knowing this was a swear word, grinned. He climbed over the fence and approached.

'Can I help?' he asked.

She stared at him. Her eyes were very strange, round and

black like coat buttons, without expression. She had a very wide mouth with thin, pale lips. Her face was an even brown with a smooth forehead going straight back into her tightly pulled-back hair.

Her mouth twitched, and the buttony eyes half-closed. '*Tu veux m'aider?*'

He blinked. It sounded so different when real French people spoke French. But he hoped he'd understood and said, '*Oui.*'

'*Avec les chèvres?*'

Ah, that's right, *chèvre* was a goat. He nodded eagerly.

'*Alors, tiens!*'

Tiens? . . . She made two fists. Hold. Oh. Hesitantly, Roger reached toward the goat's horns. It gave a strong twist of its head, then dashed away to the far side of the pen.

'*Idiot!*' she shouted. It sounded like *ee-dyo* but he guessed she meant him, not the goat.

'Sorry. Shall we catch it?'

'Eh?'

He racked his brains. '*Est-ce que nous – chasson – er – lui?*' Oh hell, this was going to be impossible. 'Don't you speak any English?' he asked despairingly.

For answer she tossed her head, and, handing him the pail and the stool, took off in quest of a goat. She caught one almost at once, and beckoned him imperiously with her head to bring her equipment. When he reached her, she grabbed the things away from him, and as good as handed him the goat.

This time he was determined not to let go. He got in front of it and grabbed its horns with both hands. It butted him in the thigh, but with its head firmly held it was helpless. He tested his strength against the goat's and found he was much stronger. It gave him a good feeling.

Next time she let him do the catching, and now she laughed at him unmercifully as he ran after two or three at once, scattering the flock in all directions. Setting his teeth, he concentrated on just one, chased it all round the pen, and

18

finally cornered it. He grabbed its horns, and dragged it back in triumph.

She was bent double, almost helpless with laughter. As she threw her head back, her small white teeth flashed in the sun.

'*Quoi est si humeureuse?*' he panted furiously.

For answer, she bent and flipped the goat's empty udder. He groaned – all that, for a goat she'd already milked! His arms dropped and the goat skipped off with a derisive twitch of its scut.

But it was funny, even he could see that. 'Well, which one then?' he asked, spreading his hands like a Frenchman.

She scanned her flock, and pointed. '*Celle-là!*'

How on earth could she remember which ones she'd done? He headed the goat straight into the corner where he'd got the other, and caught it quite efficiently this time. She rewarded him with a guarded smile, her round black eyes now shining, whether with amusement or approval he couldn't tell.

While she milked and he hung on, he asked: '*Comment tu t'appelle?*' (This came out rather well, he thought.)

'Melusine,' she answered, her forehead pressed to the goat's warm flank. '*Et toi?*'

'Roger,' he said. He heard himself give it the French pronunciation his French teacher made him use. *Prat*, he thought to himself, but it was out now.

When the pail needed emptying again, after about three goats, he followed her through the door into a dim, cool room within the stone walls of the chateau, which did duty as a dairy. Here, too, there were about one million flies.

After a little reflection he felt safe in remarking as casually as possible, '*Beaucoup de mouches.*' She nodded, lifting a muslin cover and pouring the milk into a large churn. Emboldened, he went on: '*Tu as besoin de –*' but he couldn't remember the word for frogs, which was ironic because some kids in his class called all French people frogs. If they were, there'd be a lot fewer flies! When he thought of this he couldn't help laughing, and Melusine turned to look at him.

'*Besoin de quoi?*' she asked sharply.

He decided to mime it. Crouching, he stretched his mouth with two fingers into a froggy grimace and began hopping about, snapping at the flies. She looked blank. He snapped harder. Too hard. A fly actually flew into his mouth, and he stopped hopping and snapping and spat it out.

She stared at him. She who had nearly fallen over laughing at his efforts to catch her goats for her didn't seem to see anything funny in his comic performance. He scrambled up sheepishly.

'*J'ai fini,*' she said shortly. Not a word of thanks, or even goodbye. She opened another door into the main part of the house, leaving him to find his own way back to his part around the outside. Some of the goats raised their heads as he went by, and he imagined they gave him goatish smirks.

3   Coffee from a Bowl

H is mother had already laid a ricketty old iron table
outdoors on the rough grass.

'Oh, hallo, darling, so there you are! Been exploring?' she
greeted him, emerging from the kitchen door with a tray of
bowls and plates. 'Isn't this lovely? Though I can't say I'd
call this a garden, still, the sun makes up for a lot . . .'

'*God*, these accursed flies!' Roger heard his father exclaiming from indoors. A series of exasperated whacks indicated
that he was laying about him with a rolled-up newspaper.

'Do stop doing that, Brian!' Roger's mother called. 'The
dead ones will only attract more! I swear there are fewer
outdoors than in.'

'Gotcha!' was the only answer. He appeared, examining his
kill on the newspaper with satisfaction. 'Four at a blow!'

'Brilliant,' remarked his mother. 'Keep it up, at that rate
you'll get rid of them all in about nine hundred years. Can
you bring the teapot and the marmalade?'

'Where're the twins?' asked Roger, sitting down on a rusty
garden chair and pulling the cornflakes toward him.

'Need you ask? – fast asleep. Sorry there's no proper milk.'

'Can you drink goat's milk?'

'Why do you ask?'

'Because they've got them here, loads of them.'

'Goats!' cried his father, coming out with the tea. 'So that's
it! This must be a sort of farm. I thought so from the smell,
not to mention the flies. You'd think the agency would have
mentioned that. Chateau, indeed!'

'Well, it is a real chateau,' said his mother. 'Just amazingly run-down, that's all. I wonder why.'

'Could Monsieur Serpe really be in such bad straits that he has to eke out a living as – well, as a peasant farmer? That's pretty well what he looked like, I must say. The agent said he owned the place.'

'He doesn't look like my idea of a chatelain, certainly.'

'What's that?' asked Roger.

'A chatelain's the owner of a chateau. One expects them to be rather grand, like dukes.'

Roger's father had a swig of tea, went into the flat, and returned after a moment, looking at a sheet of paper.

'"Magnificent (ha-ha) Chateau de Bois-Serpe – " well, there's the name all right " – in the heart of the Vendée, one of the most historic regions of France – "'

'What does that mean, historic regions? Is it older than unhistoric regions?' asked Roger.

His parents laughed. 'As a matter of fact, it's younger! Parts of the Vendée used to be under the sea.' Roger stopped eating and looked at his father. Was he kidding him? But he seemed quite serious. '"Historic" just means that a lot has happened here, most of it probably violent – that's what makes history, usually, is wars.' He continued reading from the sheet of paper. '"The Chateau has been in the same family for three hundred years, since pre-Revolutionary times . . ."' He read on in silence. 'Funny,' he said at last. 'It sounded so attractive when we read about it in Manchester. Perhaps anything south of Watford sounds attractive from Manchester in mid-January.' He put the paper down and reached for some Ryvita.

'Don't you like it here, then?' Roger asked rather anxiously. For some reason he wanted his parents to like it.

His father pulled down the corners of his mouth. 'It's different from expectations, somehow. Our flat's all right – '

'Our "flat", as you call it, is *gorgeous*,' said his mother firmly. 'Worth every penny to feel like a duchess for two weeks.'

'Like a chatelaine, you mean,' said his father. 'Just the same . . . I wish I'd known that our part would be the only bit of the place which hasn't been allowed to go to rack and ruin.'

'But isn't there something intriguing about that?' asked Roger's mother. 'I'll never forget the contrast between that dreadful kitchen with all its filth and squalor, and the fabulous beauty of our – *apartement*.'

'I thought that, too,' said Roger eagerly. 'I think it's very fabulous. It's got Monsieur Serpe for an ogre, and his daughter's the sort of Cinderella.'

His parents focussed attention on him.

'Have you met her – the daughter?'

'Yeah, just now.'

'What's she like? What do you mean, Cinderella?'

'Well . . . an outdoor one. She's a milkmaid.' They gazed at him expectantly. 'She milks all the goats. Dozens of them. By herself. And she knows which ones she's done, although they're all running loose.'

'Good God!' exclaimed his father.

'What?'

'The chatelain's daughter – a goat-herd! How are the mighty fallen.'

Roger frowned. He felt as if his parents were somehow looking down their noses at his new friend – if Melusine could be called that.

'How do you mean, mighty fallen?'

'It's just a way of saying that once, the family was probably pretty well-off and grand – landed gentry. I mean, if they owned all this in its heyday, and probably most of the land around here as well – and now look what they've come down to. Having to keep goats and take in summer visitors. Probably all the gracious-living stuff in our flat is the "remains of old decency" as the Irish say. They've taken every item that was any good, that had survived, and put it all together in our part of the building, and modernised it, and advertised it, and they let it out to summer visitors as a way of earning money to keep the place from falling down altogether . . . A sort of stately-home set-up. Only I should think they've left it a bit late.'

His father's long-winded explanations tended to numb Roger's concentration, but he did his best to listen this time. 'Do you mean Monsieur Serpe and Melusine were once rich?'

'I doubt it. I mean their ancestors. This place has been several generations getting into this condition.'

'What did you call her?' asked his mother.

'Melusine.'

'What an unusual name. I wonder what her sister's called.'

'Has she got a sister?'

'So the father said. She lives away from home, apparently.'

'Maybe you're right about it being an intriguing set-up,' said his father to his mother. 'I'd love to see over the place.'

Roger's father was a dentist, but his hobby was history. As Roger knew only too well. He suppressed a sigh. He hoped it wasn't going to be one of those holidays like they'd often had at home, chosen by their father for the historic associations, old buildings, museums and Roman ruins in the neighbourhood. All too seldom did one actually see something really interesting in one of these places, even though his father knew all sorts of things about everything, which occasionally struck a spark in Roger, if not in the twins.

An example of this was the little ledges in some churches called 'misericords' which old or ill monks, long ago, had been allowed to lean against to prevent them fainting during long, stand-up prayers. His father had a book of photographs of these, and some of them were extraordinarily rude, perhaps because the monks' bottoms were thought to be their unholiest bit anyway, so it didn't matter what they rested them on and the ancient wood-carvers could let their imaginations rip. But Roger still wasn't keen on the idea of enforced trips round old buildings, and he hoped the mention of this region being historic wasn't an ill omen. The bit of paper, which Roger had read in England, had also mentioned wonderful coastal beaches and a huge mass of canals somewhere near, as well as artificial lakes that you could do water sports on. He thought it rather sinister that, re-reading the agent's blurb now, his father had left all that part out.

'What about the lakes?' he asked, following this train of thought.

'H'm? Lakes?' murmured his father, who had produced a guide-book from somewhere and was reading it while eating Ryvita and marmalade. 'We must go into the village this morning,' he said to Roger's mother. 'I can't wait to get my teeth into a good *baguette* and try the local cheeses. Not to mention wine. At approximately ninety-eight p a bottle we can have some at every meal.'

This time Roger sighed without restraint. Now they were starting about food. Food was fine, but the way his parents went on about it you'd have thought it was a religion or something. Bread was bread, and cheese was cheese, and if what he'd swallowed last night in Monsieur Serpe's kitchen was a sample of the wine, he'd stick to Coke.

He stood up.

'So we won't be going to the lake or the sea today,' he said resignedly.

'Not just the first day, darling. We want to explore around here first. Don't you want to come to the village with us?'

'No, thanks. I'll hang around here.'

He picked up his empty bowl and spoon and went indoors, where he met Emma shuffling about sleepily in her nightie.

'Those rotten flies were crawling over my face,' she complained. 'They woke me up.'

'Good for them,' said Roger. 'I've been up for hours.'

'You would,' said Emma sourly, as if getting up early was a perversion of nature.

Polly, of course, was occupying the bathroom, wailing

25

because there was no hot water. She had a bath every single day, sometimes twice, and was constantly washing her hair – she was quite weird. Roger wandered through into the big room. By daylight it was even more glamorous than at night. The great octagonal table on its single stem-leg shone like a mass of jewels in the streaming sunlight. There was a big stone fireplace in here, too, with a fantastic carved stone surround, like in a baronial hall. It must be back to back with the one in the Serpes' kitchen. Roger tried the intervening door, but it was locked . . . On impulse he clambered over the stone sill of the big leaded window and moved along the outside of the building – he was in the front now – to the next window along.

He peered in through cupped hands. Yes. It was the big old ogre's-kitchen. Cobwebs and dust obscured his view, but he could see in a bit because the room ran the whole width of the chateau and there was another window the other end. There was the long table, and sitting at it were Monsieur Serpe and Melusine, eating their breakfast.

Feeling bold because he'd met her, he tapped on the window.

Monsieur Serpe leapt to his feet and spun round. Roger saw him reach out his right hand toward the fireplace, but when he saw Roger, he let it fall. Melusine was sitting looking at him. She had a bowl in both hands, which she seemed to be lifting towards her mouth. Was that how the French ate cereal? Monsieur Serpe came reluctantly and opened the window a crack.

'Bonjour, Monsieur!' said Roger hopefully.

'*Qu'est-ce que tu veux?*' growled the man.

'*Puis-je – er – entrer?*'

'*On mange maintenant,*' he answered in a surly tone, and turned on his heel. But he didn't close the window, and Roger threw his leg over the sill and climbed in.

The first thing he noticed was a gun, a heavy hunting rifle, leaning against the stone front of the fireplace. So that was what Monsieur Serpe had been reaching for! Roger had better watch out. With the ogre, it might be a question of shooting first and asking questions later.

He sat down gingerly on a hard chair, its seat blackened with the grime of years, next to Melusine.

'Hallo,' he said shyly.

She glanced at him out of her round eyes. The bowl, he saw, was full of milky coffee, and she was dipping the rounded end of a very thin crusty white loaf into it.

'*Tu veux du café?*'

He didn't think he did, but he was pleased she'd offered and said, '*Oui, merci.*'

She got up and fetched another of the thick blue-striped bowls, and poured milky coffee into it from a huge jug. Then she broke off a stick of bread for him. He dipped it, and bent to catch the soggy part in his mouth. To his surprise it was perfectly delicious. Watching what she did, he took the bowl in both hands. It felt lovely and smooth and hot. He carried it to his mouth and drank the stuff.

'*Bon!*' he exclaimed appreciatively, emerging with a coffee moustache. Some of it had spilled on his T-shirt. She suddenly smiled, picked up a filthy dishcloth and wiped his front.

'I'm not used to drinking from a bowl,' he explained. '*En Angleterre, nous buvons d'une tasse. Pas une* – one of these,' he pointed.

She laughed, showing her pointed tongue.

Monsieur Serpe, who had been watching them, finished the meal in silence and then got up and left. Melusine stood up, too, and began collecting the most recently-used dishes.

A most useful French word now popped into Roger's head – it had been in the last vocabulary he'd had to learn before the end-of-year tests. It was the word for 'washing-up'. '*Puis-je vous aider avec les vaisselles?*' he asked carelessly.

She understood! She shook her head, and carried the dishes to a distant sink. It was not like the stainless steel ones Roger was used to. It was a deep white thick one, big enough to wash a goat in. She started rinsing the bowls rather carelessly under the crude splash of the one, presumably cold, tap, a big old brass one. Roger sidled up behind her, preparing a French sentence.

'*Je veux voir le château*,' he said hopefully.

She turned and gave him an odd look. He thought she was pleased he wanted to see the place. But then her face closed, and she turned away.

'*Rien à voir.*'

Nothing to see? 'There must be,' he said. '*C'est si grand – il y a beaucoup des chambres, n'est-ce pas?*'

'*Fermées.*'

'*Toutes les autres chambres fermées?*' he asked disbelievingly. This was obviously a put-off. They must *sleep* somewhere, for a start.

She hesitated. '*Peut-être qu'elles ne sont pas toutes fermées. Mais . . .*'

Roger waited. After a moment, when she didn't go on, he flushed awkwardly and said, 'It's okay then, "san fairy ann",' which was what his grandfather used to say when he meant 'It doesn't matter.'

Melusine licked her lips, turned back to the sink, stacked the bowls, without drying them, on to a shelf, and suddenly electrified him by announcing:

'I show you one big room. *Et puis, fini!*'

His face broke into a great grin.

'You speak English!'

'Very, very bad. *Viens alors!*'

Roger had to restrain himself from jumping about with pleasure. Melusine was already leaving the room. He followed her, marvelling at the way she moved. He hadn't noticed it in the goat-pen this morning because of the uneven ground. Now as she walked ahead of him down the stone corridor it was as if she glided on wheels, into the shadows, and at the corner – vanished.

He hurried after her.

28

4   The Tour

Roger followed the girl for what seemed like miles through badly-lit passages. At what he judged to be the middle of the building, they crossed a vast open hall with another huge fireplace, elaborately carved, and a magnificent flight of stairs, but no furniture whatever. She gave him no time to stop and stare, but glided straight on through more passages, and at last stopped before a pair of double doors which she flung open.

'*Voilà. Le grand salon,*' she said, with sarcastic indifference.

He stopped in the doorway, gazing round. Everything his father had said at breakfast came into focus and made sense. This must once have been a ballroom, full of life, light and magnificence.

Like the hall, it was huge; like the hall, stripped of everything that might have made it into a room people lived in, instead of just an echoing empty space. All there was left to show what it had once been, was head-high oak panelling and a high ceiling with the faded traces of paintings on it. The floor-boards stretched so far away into the distance that they almost came to a point at the far wall. The dust was so thick everywhere that it was like looking at the room through a piece of tracing-paper.

It was, in general, dull and disappointing. Even his father, Roger felt, with his passion for the human history in old buildings, couldn't find anything interesting to look at here.

He turned back to Melusine, who was watching him with a rather cynical expression which was oddly grown-up.

'*Satisfait?*'

'Isn't there anything more interesting than this?'

'*Des chambres fermées. Des chambres vides.* That is interesting?'

'No.'

'I say you. *Rien à voir.*' She drew him out of the doorway and closed the door with a bang.

They walked in silence till they came back into the big hall. This was where the main front door of the chateau was. It had a big fanlight over it, and locks and bolts on the inside. It didn't look as if it had been opened for centuries. The floor was flagged, like Roger's room, only these were lovely silvery-grey ones, polished by the feet of many generations in better times, now dull with disuse. Roger paused by the foot of the great stairway.

'Can we go up here?'

He saw Melusine was about to say no. Then she shrugged. His interest returning, he bounded up the curving, shallow stairs three at a time while she followed more sedately.

They spent the next half-hour rattling the doorhandles of the 'chambres fermées' and peering into the 'chambres vides'. There were an incredible number of both, but there was nothing else remarkable and Roger would have got bored much sooner except that being with Melusine was interesting in itself. They managed to work up quite a conversation, between his awful French and her awful English, and she began to unbend a little.

He asked her bluntly if she and her father had ever been rich. She shook her head.

'We have no money. Never we have money. *Mon oncle* he has our money *mais il est au Canada.*'

'Did he steal it? *Voleur?*'

'No. Is his money.'

'You said it was yours.'

'He is – big from my papa.'

'He begged it?' said Roger, frowning.

'No! Big!' She indicated height with her hand.

30

'Oh, I see! You mean he's older than your father.'

She nodded. 'My papa he has the chateau. *Mon oncle*, he has the money.'

'That seems silly.'

'Silly. *Oui*. So think my papa also.'

They looked idly into a few more empty rooms. The sunlight, falling through the dust-motes on to the bare floors, began to call Roger to come outdoors.

'Let's go out.'

He was quite lost by now, but Melusine led the way unerringly along the passages. Suddenly Roger noticed that, as they turned a corner, the wall on his left was oddly curved.

'Is this the tower?' he asked with renewed eagerness.

'*Quoi?*'

'*La tour.*'

There was a door, a curved one to match the wall, and his hand went out to its handle, but with a sudden striking movement almost too fast to see, she lashed out, knocking it away.

'Ow!' he shouted. 'That hurt!'

'*Pardon,*' she muttered sullenly. But then she looked up at him. There was a fierce light in her black eyes as she said: 'You go not there. *C'est défendu, tu comprends?*'

'Okay, okay!'

She walked on, paused, turned back.

'I am sorry,' she said. '*Je t'ai fait mal?*' She lifted his hand and examined the red mark on his wrist.

He felt the touch of her hand oddly – it was cool, a little rough from her work, yet at the same time it was both warm and smooth. How it could seem both at once, he didn't know, but it sent a shiver up his arm and he almost snatched his hand away from her, saying, 'No, it's okay! Come on, let's get out of here. The dust's making my throat tickle.'

He met his family for a late lunch. By this time it was too hot to eat out. His mother clearly had not felt it possible to spread a simple meal of French bread, butter, Brie cheese, pâté, pears and wine on the magnificent inlaid table in the big room. They ate in homely fashion in the kitchen, much to the disgust of Emma and Polly.

'Well when *can* we use that room?' asked Polly, kicking the leg of the wooden table fretfully. 'It's horrible in here where the doors have been open all the morning and let all the flies in.'

'Oh, do shut up about the flies, Poll,' said their father cheerfully. He was in a very good mood after several glasses of wine. 'Look at the weather! You should go outside where the flies won't bother you, like Roger.'

Polly gave him a sour look.

'Where have you been all morning, anyhow?' asked Emma, toying unenthusiastically with the pâté.

'I've been exploring,' said Roger.

'On your own?'

'Most of the time.' He bit hungrily into his bread. It was so crisply fresh that large flakes of crust flew everywhere.

'Weren't you with Melusine?' asked their mother 'I saw – '

She was drowned out by a duet of hoots from the twins.

'*Melusine!*' they shrieked. 'What a name! It sounds like floor polish!'

'No, like a brand of gooey cheese – like this yuk.'

'Be quiet, girls! Don't be so silly, it's a beautiful French name, probably local, wouldn't you say, Brian?'

'God, this is good,' responded their father, eating cheese and pear in alternate bites. 'I could live on this. Shall we open another bottle?'

'She had to do some holiday homework,' said Roger. 'So we just went and checked that the goats were okay, and then I went off on my own.'

'Oh, so she does go to school?'

'Of course. Why shouldn't she? She's only about my age.'

His mother got up to fetch another loaf. 'It's just that –

well, I don't know. This place is so isolated. And they seem so – '

'What?' asked Roger, beginning to bristle. If she said 'primitive' he was prepared to be angry.

His mother was watching him. She sensed his feelings sometimes.

'She looks so – grown-up, as if – but I suppose that's because she keeps house for her father. Silly of me, of course she goes to school. Does she speak English?'

'Sort of. She said she's going to work at it now we're here.'

'Oooooh,' chorused the twins mockingly. 'So she can chat up Rodge!'

'Shut up,' said Roger automatically.

His mind wasn't on them. He was thinking about his secret discovery. After he'd left Melusine, he'd found traces of the drive which had once led up to the front of the house. He'd realized there must have been one, because, about half a mile away, in a line with the front door, he'd seen two great stone gateposts standing up all by themselves in a field. There was no wall, and no gate. Very strange they'd looked, like two giant soldiers turned to stone centuries ago, still guarding the house in its time of decay just as they had in what his father had called its hey-day.

Roger had walked out to them, straight, stumbling over clumps of weed and pushing through seedlings which had grown up in the way. He'd felt the ground extra hard and knobbly under his sandals, and cleared a bit of the earth and grass with a stick, and found the remains of the drive underneath – cobbles, like an old Roman road.

He knew his father would like it. He would show it to him when he was ready. He wasn't ready yet. He didn't even want to tell anyone about his trip round the chateau. He didn't know why. It had something to do with not being allowed to go into the tower. Melusine had been very firm about it – very firm indeed! Roger rubbed his wrist reminiscently. But

33

that was not the end of it with him. He meant to get her to take him up there. Or to get up there himself, somehow.

It was really too hot to do anything after lunch, so Roger retreated to his little larder-bedroom. To his pleased surprise, it was beautifully cool, and flyless. Also dark, but that didn't matter. He lay down on his camp bed and fell asleep – quite blissfully. He hadn't realized that after-lunch sleeps, or siestas as his parents called them, were somehow different from night-sleeps. About an hour later, when he woke up, he knew he had something he wanted to do, something he hadn't thought he would want to do at all during the holiday. He got off the bed and pulled his suitcase out from under it. One of the things he had not unpacked or put on the shelf was his parcel of school books. His mother had made them all bring holiday work. He certainly hadn't meant to even look at it until she made him but now he took the parcel out and emptied the books and notebooks on the bed.

Among them was a small French-English dictionary, and his French text. He also selected a notebook and pencil. Then he brushed the rest back into his suitcase, turned on the light, lay back on the bed again, and began to attack his French.

5 Learning to Milk

By milking time Roger had learnt an astonishing amount of French, or rather re-learnt it: he'd never really tried before.

Arriving at the goat-pen ahead of Melusine, he practised his catching technique on a goat or two, and then he had an idea. There was some coarse string in shortish lengths hanging from a hook in the dairy – he'd noticed it this morning. He went in there and got some, and tucked it into the top of his shorts. Then he caught a goat, tied a piece of string to one of its horns and attached it loosely to the fence. It tugged furiously once or twice, but he hastily pulled some grass from outside the fence and put it on the ground. The goat began to eat and forgot it was tied.

Roger then pulled lots of grass till he had a fairly big heap. He stung his hands on some hidden nettles but that didn't stop him. He strewed the grass in a line on the inside of the fence and then set about his self-appointed task.

By the time Melusine emerged through the dairy door, there were five goats tied up and munching, waiting to be milked.

She stopped short and stared at the tethered goats. Her face was a blank. He simply couldn't tell if she were pleased or angry, and he was annoyed to find his heart thumping as if in fear. But abruptly she turned, disappeared back into the dairy, emerged with her stool and pail, and, crossing the pen, took up her milking position beside the first of his goats.

'*Puis-je essayer de traire?*' he asked.

Her face was hidden, pressed to the goat's flank. The milk dringed steadily into the pail. After a moment she muttered: 'What is *traire* in English?'

'To milk.'

'You want to milk?'

'*Oui.*'

'It is hard to do it.'

'Let me just try. *Essayer.*'

After another moment she moved aside, still holding the pail, and he took her place on the three-legged stool. It didn't feel very secure, and he felt strange and uncomfortable. She took his kneecaps in her smooth-rough, warm-cold hands and pressed them against the sides of the pail. Then, without touching the goat, she showed him how to squeeze with a downwards movement, the top fingers squeezing first and the little fingers last. He tried the movement a few times in the air, and at last she indicated that he might take hold of the teats.

They were hot and rubbery and touching them made him shudder with a strange disgust at first. The goat was equally disgusted – it lifted its head from the grass and he felt it half-crouch as if it meant to kick him. But Melusine held its head and spoke to it while he tried to put her lesson into practice. He squeezed, he pulled, he did everything he knew, including *will* the milk to emerge, but absolutely not a drop did.

Finally he got so frustrated he just let himself slump off the stool backwards into the mucky straw.

'Grrrragh!' he shouted. '*C'est impossible!*' The worst was, she would laugh at him again. But this time she didn't.

'*Ce n'est pas impossible, mais c'est difficile. Regardes moi.*'

She bent and showed him, moving her fingers very slowly and strongly, drawing the milk down the teat with a sinuous movement of her hand that reminded him of something swallowing. It was fascinating. His hand went to the second teat and he copied her exactly. And suddenly he felt the milk, felt how he had to draw it down from the bag into the teat,

36

and on down, and out – and out it came! Only a little squirt, but it trickled into the bucket beside Melusine's steady stream.

Excited, he pushed her aside, resumed his seat on the stool, and tried again with both hands. It *was* hard, but little by little he began to get the knack. At each squeeze a tiny amount of milk came out, and after a while, just a little more. When Melusine wanted to take over from him, he wouldn't give way. He was determined to finish at least one goat down to the last drop. But after a few more minutes his hands began to ache, the skin on his index fingers to smart. The goat stamped her hoof and tossed her head irritably. And suddenly he got up . . . It wasn't that he couldn't go on a bit longer, but if his fingers were hurting, what about the goat? She was used to being milked in *four minutes!*

He watched Melusine expertly strip the last drops. And when she looked up at him with the trace of a smile on her face, he grinned across his red and sweating one and said:

'*Je peux traire! N'est-ce pas?*'

And she nodded once, and replied: '*Oui, bien sûr.*'

He felt as if she'd pinned a medal on him.

When he got in for supper, Emma said: 'Phew! You stink!'

'Shut up,' said Roger.

'You are a bit high, darling,' said their mother. 'And – good grief, Roger, look at the seat of your shorts! What have you been sitting in?'

'Goat shit,' said Roger.

Fortunately his mother was not too fussy about Anglo-Saxon words, at least when used in their correct context and not as abuse, so she merely said drily, 'Rather you than me. Go and change.'

'And have a shower!' Emma called after him.

He met Polly coming out of the bathroom with wet hair. She too made a face and exaggeratedly held her nose.

'Phew, you stink!' she said.

They weren't twins for nothing, even though they were not

identical. They were always together and their minds seemed to work as one – certainly about Roger, against whom they had ganged up practically from the moment they were born. He certainly couldn't remember a time when he had not felt that, basically, it was a case of two against one.

Yet he seemed to remember that when they were all younger, before he became a teenager, there had been long periods of truce during which they had managed to play together, support each other (occasionally) at school and in the streets while playing out, and even put their natural hostility aside sometimes to become a three-person team. He had almost liked them then. Now his philosophical thoughts about them were limited to asking himself from time to time which of them he loathed more.

His usual ploy was to ignore them, and he did this with Polly now, brushing past her and shutting himself into the steamy bathroom. Actually it was a shower-room. Roger had never had a shower before, not a real, no-bath one. Polly had complained bitterly at lunch about it, and their father had said it was far cleaner, quicker and more economic than bathing ('sitting in your own dirty water') and that he was seriously thinking of installing a shower at home. The girls had set up their invariable caterwauling at the prospect of any change from what they were used to, but Roger liked to think he was more flexible. He stripped off his clothes, adjusted the heat of the water, turned the handle on to full, and stepped into the shallow tiled square, drawing the plastic curtains around him.

The minute he was in there and felt the warm water pouring over him from head to foot he knew showers were for him. The gentle impact of the separate streams could be individually felt on his face. He soaped himself all over and watched all the foam and dirt (there was a lot of both) being carried down his body and vanishing down the plughole. He saw at once exactly what his father meant. Fancy all that muck being still in the bathwater, with you soaking in it! This was much, much better.

He wondered suddenly if Melusine had a shower. When this thought occurred to him, a picture came into his mind of her body, straight and slim with her strange face turned upward to the shower-head, her black hair wet and loose around her shoulders. The details were blurred by the spray as if she were veiled. He shook his head sharply like a dog coming out of a river and the picture went away.

He stayed under the shower for ages, he liked it so much. Finally his father came and banged on the door.

'Don't you want your supper? Come on!'

He came out reluctantly, put on clean clothes and slid into his chair at the kitchen table. Supper was soup from a tin and the French bread, by now gone completely crisp, like a rusk.

'How did you get yourself into such a mess?' asked his father cheerfully.

'I was milking the goats.'

The girls looked at him.

'You don't know how,' said Emma.

'Yes, I do,' he said mildly. 'Melusine taught me.' He waited for them to jeer at him in the mindless way they usually did if he even mentioned a girl's name, but this time they didn't.

'Good for her,' said his father. 'And good for you, son. I learnt to milk at about your age, when I spent a summer on a farm. It was cows, though, not goats.' He flexed his hands rememberingly. 'It takes for ever to strip a Jersey cow's udders.' The girls sniggered idiotically, and for once he turned on them. 'Don't be so silly, you two! There's nothing funny about a cow's udders, let me tell you. And there's nothing easy about milking them. I had blisters on my hands for the first week. Did she give you some ointment to put on your hands before you started?'

'No.'

'I had to rub lashings of this thick white gunge into my hands to help them slip properly on the teats – '

At this, both girls broke into explosions of ill-suppressed mirth. Emma threw up her hands to her mouth to catch a spray of soup. Polly practically fell under the table.

'Teats!' they wheezed. 'Teats . . .'

'I am going to hit them in a minute,' remarked their father quite matter-of-factly to their mother. 'So you'd better stop them making that imbecile row.'

'Leave the table, both of you,' said their mother.

Instead they made a noble effort to pull themselves together. It wasn't an outstanding success but at least they tried.

Roger went on talking to his father as best he could through the snorts and snuffles.

'I wasn't very good. I couldn't even finish one goat, and it's only two te – it's much less work than a cow, obviously. But I did do one thing that helped.' And he told about his system with the tethers. While Melusine had milked the other four goats he'd already caught, he caught and tethered a new lot. Then, while she worked her way steadily down the line, he released the milked ones. He was thinking while he did it. He could not see how she knew which ones she'd milked already from the dozens frisking about in the big pen – he certainly couldn't. If he was going to help her, it would be better if they had another pen to release the finished goats into. Or perhaps a sort of paling which you could fix up temporarily across part of the main pen.

He explained this to his father, who listened with great seriousness.

'That shouldn't present any problems, provided you can find some hurdles, or, failing that, just a couple of ropes stretched across would keep them in for the short time you'd need. Maybe I'll stroll round and – ' But then he became aware that his wife was giving him eye-signals and he stopped. 'No. Quite right. This is your territory, Roger, you can solve it, I'm sure. You'll no doubt revolutionise the system.'

In bed that night, Roger gave the matter some thought.

40

Rope was a good idea, obviously the simplest solution. There was quite a long piece of rope coiled in the boot of the car for emergencies. He'd get up early in the morning and try it out before she arrived.

Just as he was dropping off, his eyes snapped open. It was a faint enough sound, but he couldn't identify it. A sort of crinkly rustle, a little like the sound his mother made when she rubbed a ball of old tissue paper over a windowpane to clean it, only that it didn't go to and fro, it just went softly, whisperingly on and on. After a little while, and before he could exactly decide where it was in the room, it stopped. It was only when it stopped, that Roger realized that he had been holding his breath and that the hairs on the back of his neck were bristling. He thought he ought to get up, turn the light on and search the room, but he didn't.

It took him a long time to get to sleep after that.

6   The Oriental Charmer

It was a glorious morning. When Roger came out (leaving all his family fast asleep) he saw that a pale gold mist lay over the fields beyond the line of trees. There was another line of what looked like huge, gnarled old willows, some distance away; Roger wondered if there were a river there. He liked rivers; there was always something interesting to do around a river.

The stone giants – the ancient gateposts – stood, as it were, knee-deep in milky mist. One of them had a slight list, where one side of it, unsupported now by gate or wall, had settled into the earth, so it was no longer straight as sentries should be. As Roger, carrying the coil of rope, crossed over where the drive had been and turned his head to look at them, he thought they looked rather sad in the golden morning light, their function gone, just waiting there for nothing except to fall down . . . Such a notion was unusual for him. He thought it silly, usually, to ascribe human feelings to objects.

When Melusine saw the roped-off area she at once understood what it was for.

'*Bonne idée*,' she said, enthusiastically for her.

Roger grinned happily, and, for a change, she grinned back. Her button eyes half closed with the grin, and this made them look more ordinary, and much nicer. It changed her whole face in a way that her laugh – which he associated, till now, with mockery – didn't.

He was allowed to milk the first goat, and this time he got

nearly all the milk out, though it took a long time and the goat got fed up. After that he resumed his catching and tethering duties, hurrying back every so often to release the goats as she finished them. He got them into the roped-off section by the simple tactic of raising the rope, which was chest-high to the goats, and shoving them underneath it.

'*Combien de temps* – er – *prends-tu, en général, de laire* – er – *toutes les chèvres?*' he asked.

'*A peu près une heure et demie.*'

He had glanced at his watch before she started. When she finished, he glanced at it again. Just over three-quarters of an hour!

'*Tu m'as gagné beaucoup de temps,*' she acknowledged as she carried the last pailful into the cool dairy. '*Merci.*'

'So now will you show me the tower?' he asked, quick to take advantage of her mellow mood.

She spun round, her eyes round and unreadable again. '*Quoi?*'

She'd understood all right, but to make sure, he said, '*Je veux voir la tour.*'

Again he saw that she was about to give him a short, angry reply. But she stifled it. She turned away, poured the milk into the churn, covered it with the lid, and carried the pail out to wash under a standpipe tap. He followed her closely to show the question was still hanging.

'Well?' he pressed. '*Qu'est-ce que tu dis?*'

She stood very still, turned away from him. Then she turned and smiled.

'Maybe. But no today. Today I going with my father.'

'Where?'

'To La Rochelle.'

'Ah,' said Roger wisely, having no idea where that was. But he lost no time in finding out. There was a map of France in the glove-pocket of the car, and a few minutes after saying 'adieu' to Melusine he had this spread out over the bonnet.

43

The first place he looked – wishful thinking – was the coast. And immediately he found it. It was a town west of them, about one hour, he reckoned, by a rather good road. Right on the sea. And, when he looked at the more detailed map of the Vendée region that his father had brought, he saw that just north of the town was what looked like a long beach.

'Could we go to the coast today?' he asked carelessly at breakfast.

'*Yes!*' chorused the twins, who after one day with nothing special to do were practically paralysed with boredom.

'I don't know why not,' said their father. 'I thought we'd look into the canal situation first, they're closer, but it's such a good day, perhaps the sea would be nice – '

'Could you face another long drive so soon?' asked their mother. 'Because, if you liked – *I* don't mind – '

'No, no,' said their father hurriedly. 'I'll drive. You make the picnic.'

Roger could never understand why it took grown-ups so incredibly long to get ready for an outing. For his part, he sorted out and put back in the car the blow-up dinghy, pump, and paddles, and the flippers and snorkels, and checked that the rug and folding chairs were in. Then he fetched a towel and rolled his bathing trunks in it, clapped a species of hat on his head before his mother had a chance to tell him to, and he was ready. But of course no one else was, so he slipped away round the front of the chateau in the hope of finding out when Melusine was leaving.

The big front window of the kitchen was ajar and he scrambled in as he had done the morning before. He felt this was all right since Monsieur Serpe had seen him do it and not reproved him. The kitchen was empty. Even by day it was very dark and somehow threatening, when there was no one in it.

Roger noticed that the gun had been taken away. He wondered if Monsieur Serpe went shooting for game. Roger

44

had never tasted game and was rather unsure what it was, exactly (he used to think the phrase was 'shooting for *a* game') – but he'd tasted, done and seen so many new things since coming to France, he was more than game for some game if anyone should offer him any. He wouldn't mind, he thought, having a shot at some, either, but both his parents had flatly refused to entertain the idea of buying a gun for him.

He moved round the room idly, letting his eyes rove about, but apart from a couple of dark brown ham-like things hanging from the rafters (smoked goat-haunch?) together with strings of dried mushrooms and bunches of withered leaves and a long, long rope of white garlic, beautifully plaited, there was really nothing at all interesting. Everything was covered with layers of dirt, except one end of the long table, where the oil-cloth had been kept wiped. To amuse himself, Roger counted the items carelessly strewn about the table. He'd reached thirty-seven and was wondering whether to count the rusty screws and nails as individuals or just a spilt tinful, when a voice behind him nearly made him jump out of his skin.

'*Qu'est-ce que tu fais là?*'

He spun round, his heart thumping.

It was the ogre, of course. And there was the gun, in both hands – not quite pointing at Roger, but definitely at the ready, and his question had been more like a snarl. Roger found himself backed against the table, looking at Monsieur Serpe's menacing figure lurking in the shadows near the outer door.

All his French deserted him. 'I – I – I'm sorry, I – I was looking for Melusine,' he stammered.

The man began to shout at him. Roger couldn't understand a word, but he got the message: 'Get out and stay out!' He lost no time. He ran to the window and scrambled out as fast as he could go, falling down into the grass outside and for a few seconds lying there, winded, as if someone had hit him in the stomach.

Then he got up and ran to the window of their own big room.

From there he could hear the car horn blasting. He stumbled, panting, round to the back of the chateau to find them all ready to leave, furious with him for keeping them waiting.

He managed to calm down quite quickly in the car, without telling anyone what had happened. By the time they'd reached La Rochelle he'd practically forgotten about it.

La Rochelle was quite a big town. It had an old part and a new part. The old part was the port, next to the sea, and its cobbled roads and masses of little shops and cafés were potentially quite interesting, but not half as interesting to Roger and the twins just then as the beach. It was great, super sand and waves just right for jumping but not too high to launch the dinghy. Their parents wouldn't let them use it on the ocean if it were at all rough, not after Emma, the twit, had allowed herself to be carried away by the current at Newport, on one of their Welsh holidays, and had to be rescued by some fellows in a motorboat.

They had an unblemished afternoon, quite a rarity, really. No grouses or sniping from the girls, no nagging or bellowing from parents; no chill half-hours of sunlessness, no sand in the picnic, even, and his dad in a highly benign mood which meant ice-creams without stint and plenty of co-operation with pumping up, and later patching, the dinghy.

Roger did look around from time to time to see if Melusine and her father might be anywhere about, but he didn't really expect to see them. Who could imagine the ogre in bathing-trunks disporting himself on a beach like a human being? Roger found it difficult to imagine even Melusine just messing around having fun.

By four o'clock they'd run out of picnic food and had had enough of the beach. They got dressed, packed up and between them carted all the stuff back up to the car, always

46

the worst part of any day out, especially the dinghy, which resisted deflation and was heavy with water and stuck-on sand.

'Here, Em, you take the other end.'

'No, I can't. I'm carrying all the towels.'

'All the towels! You're carrying *your* towel.'

'Well, it's heavy.'

'Just because you took the biggest . . . Take the paddles, at least.'

'What's wrong with you taking them? You could carry them under your other arm.'

'Poll, you give us a hand then, eh?'

'Me? I'm carrying the chairs!'

'Carry them both in one hand and hold the dinghy with the other!' shouted Roger in exasperation. His good mood with his sisters had evaporated during this short exchange, just as it always did when they tried to get away with doing as little as possible.

He stumped off after his parents with the pump and paddles somehow clutched in one hand and arm, dragging the damned dinghy after him across the sand and then across the stones. Of course his father had to turn round and tell him not to drag it if he didn't want it to get more punctures. The twins followed, lightly burdened and beginning to quarrel. Roger set his teeth. It looked like being a ghastly drive back.

The idea had been to load up the car and start the drive home, to avoid any risk of arriving after dark. The chateau, located in the remote countryside between two villages, was quite hard to find even by day, along the maze of cart-tracks that led to it. But suddenly their father decided that they had half an hour to spare and that the grown-ups should perhaps have a coffee or a glass of wine in the old port, to fortify them for the journey.

'Can we have some chips?' asked Roger.

'Be satisfied with all that ice-cream,' said his father, his benign mood abruptly a thing of the past. 'Don't be such an

47

Oliver.' This reference to Oliver Twist's habit of asking for more was a family watchword, most unfairly applied in this case, Roger thought. He resented it, as whatever he was, he wasn't greedy. He felt himself begin to sink into something like a sulk, which would really ruin the day good and proper if he didn't yank himself out of it. But sometimes he couldn't.

This might well have been one of those times, except that, as they were wandering through the narrow streets and old-fashioned squares of the port, looking for a bar, Roger suddenly saw Melusine.

She was standing by herself near the front of a small crowd, watching two street entertainers. They were a young man and woman, dressed crazily in all sorts of bright-coloured clothes, with lots of funny make-up on. The woman wore a turban, and she was pretending to be an Indian snake-charmer. The man was the snake. He was crouching in a basket, doing a weaving sort of dance while she played a flute.

Roger drew the family to a halt and they all watched and joined in the laughter and applause. But Roger was watching Melusine more than the act. She hadn't seen him. She seemed not to have eyes for anything except the girl who was playing the music. She played very well, not just 'tootling'. Later, Roger's father was to say the two were probably music students trying to eke out their grant. And it was the right kind of music, very Eastern-sounding, not just phoney Eastern either, but the real thing. And Melusine was moving to the notes, not dancing but swaying, writhing her shoulders and arms, swaying her hips, her head making figures of eight on her neck ... Her eyes, round and black, stared through everything, fixed on the flute. Her mouth was slightly open, her tongue between her lips ... Her whole body seemed possessed and commanded by the thin, high notes.

And Roger felt their power, too, or *some* power. For a timeless moment he felt what it was like to be hypnotized. Only it was much more Melusine who hypnotized him, not the music itself. His family, the crowd, the actors, the square

– they all faded away into a sort of golden mist, like the river-mist that had covered the ground that morning. Only Melusine, her wreathing, swaying movements, her staring eyes, remained real and effective to him. 'Watching' was not an intense enough word for what he did to her. He drank her with his eyes. He knew that if she turned and beckoned to him, he would have to cross the open space between them and go to her.

Suddenly he came to himself. Something had interfered with his trance. It was his mother, nudging him.

'Look, Roger! There's Melusine!'

He felt himself break into a sweat and begin to shiver. He forced himself to answer, as naturally as possible, 'Yes, I saw her.'

'What *is* she doing?'

'She's doing a snake dance better than the "snake"!' said his father. 'Come on, this is boring. Let's have our drink and get on our way.'

7   *The Stone Head*

Roger was car-sick on the way back. This was practically unheard-of, and even the twins were nice to him – well, he had managed not to throw up inside the car, for which they were probably quite grateful; when Polly had used be car-sick, she never bothered to ask for the car to be stopped, so they all knew what the alternative was.

After Roger had crawled back into the car, feeling somewhat better but still pretty fragile, Emma sat in the middle without being told to so that he could have the outside place near the window. She even put an arm round him and addressed him in unusually gentle tones.

'Wod pooh Wodder feeding wodden, den? Wodder wanda pudden head on Eddy's solder?'

It was an indication of her concern for him that she spoke to him in Woddy, the language of their childhood which consisted largely of D's, O's and W's. It was only used between them now on the increasingly rare occasions when they were feeling fond of each other and wanted to say something soppy which they naturally couldn't say in their normal voices. When spoken fast enough, Woddy was still a secret language incomprehensible to their 'Dod' and 'Mod', which made its non-sentimental use also occasionally desirable.

But now it meant only that Emma was genuinely sorry for him. And he felt sorry for himself, to tell the truth. It was so unusual for him to feel all woozy and sick. Maybe it was having two rather scary experiences in one day. Before he drifted off to sleep with his head on Emma's shoulder he asked himself why watching Melusine moving to the snake-charm music should have frightened him. He had no answer.

Melusine's father must have known a quicker way home than Roger's, because by the time they got back the Serpes' vehicle – an old heap of a farm pickup – was already standing outside the back of the chateau. Roger, who felt much better after his sleep, hurried round to the goat-pen to find Melusine half-way through the milking, using the old, random-catch system in his absence.

He stood some distance behind her, looking at her critically. She looked just as she had when he'd first seen her, her black pigtail hanging down to her waist, the diamond-pattern T-shirt now badly in need of a wash. . . . She'd had time to change, then, since getting back from La Rochelle. What had she been wearing there? . . . He couldn't remember. Something green . . . He screwed up his eyes, remembering her as she had stood in the square. She had looked different. But now she looked the way he knew her best, and it was easy to forget she had scared him and just climb the fence and creep up behind her.

'Boo!'

But she didn't even twitch. She must have heard him coming, despite all the noise the goats were making.

'Hallo,' she said calmly without looking round. 'How you are? Where you are be?'

'I are be in La Rochelle, same as you,' Roger said. 'I saw you.'

Her whole body jerked, and the bucket tottered. He bent and grabbed it to steady it, and their hands, seizing its rim at the same place, touched. He looked into her face. It was white.

'What's the matter? *Qu'est-ce qu'il y a?*'

'*Rien! Laisse-moi!*' she almost shouted in a shrill voice.

He let go the pail and stood up.

51

'I was only trying to help,' he said. He felt hurt, really hurt that she'd spoken to him like that. She put her head against the goat's flank and went on milking while he stood there. There was a silence between them. He felt like just walking away, but he didn't. Instead he said, 'So what if I saw you?'

'Where I was that you see me?' she asked, in a muffled tone.

'In that little square. You were sort of dancing.'

'*Quoi?*'

He couldn't think of the word for dance, so he did a clumsy imitation of her swaying movements, trying to make a joke of it. She stared at him, her mouth open, her round eyes wide so that he could see the whites all round the black irises.

'*I* do like this?'

'Of course. You remember. The girl played – ' he mimed the flute ' – and you danced.' And he wiggled his hips and tried to make the figure-of-eight movement with his head.

Suddenly she jumped up, snatching up the pail, and faced him. He was horrified to see that tears had sprung into his eyes.

'*Tu mens! Je n'ai pas fait ça! Jamais! Jamais!*'

And, turning, she ran away from him into the dairy, leaving the stool on its side in the straw. Roger stood stunned for a moment. Had she dared to call him a liar? But when he picked up the pail and went after her with it, he found the dairy door bolted from the inside. Putting his ear to it, he was shocked to hear her sobbing.

'Melusine!' he called sharply. She was frightening him again, in quite a different way this time. 'Open the door!' He banged on it with his fist. '*Ouvrez la porte!*' The sobbing stopped. He banged again, commandingly, the way his mother occasionally banged on the twins' door at home when they'd locked themselves in. It was a knock which demanded that the door be opened. And sure enough, after a subdued rustling of straw, the top part of the door was opened a little and Melusine's sullen, tear-stained face appeared.

52

'Let me in,' he said shortly.

The lower half was unbolted and he walked into the half-dark, milk-and-goat-smelling room. Melusine stood aside. She hung her head and looked limp and submissive, not like her. It made him feel strange, as if he'd done something so awful to her that he'd defeated her, somehow. He wanted to put his arm round her, as Emma had with him, in the car. But he sensed she would flinch away if he tried. Instead he went and sat down on a bench and said,

'Please come here.'

She came slowly, dragging her feet. He noticed that she wore leather boots, laced to her ankles, old and cracked, without socks. Her legs were scratched and muddy. The sight disturbed him, because they looked like a boy's legs, except that they definitely weren't. They made him feel suddenly terribly sorry for her, even more than her tears.

He patted the bench beside him and she sat down, not looking at him, wiping her wet face with the palms of her hands, leaving smears.

'What's wrong? What did I say wrong?'

She sniffed.

'I not do like you say. No, never.'

He opened his mouth to contradict her, then shut it again.

'Okay,' he said. 'I must have just thought it was you.'

She gave him half a smile and then looked down into her lap again. They sat for some time in silence. The sun sent a beam in through the top of the door, so bright and square and full of dust it looked solid.

Outside the goats bleated, and inside the flies whined. Several flies landed on them, but only Roger brushed them away. Melusine sat motionless as if she were asleep, while the flies crawled over her knees. It was weird. . . . After a while he stood up. He picked up the pail and emptied it into the churn.

'Come on,' he said. 'We'd better finish the milking.'

* * *

At supper that night, Roger's father said, 'Today we went on a you-lot outing. Tomorrow we're going on a me-outing.'

The twins groaned.

'Oh *no!* It's churches, isn't it?'

'It is indeed. This area's stiff with 'em, marvellous Romanesque ones . . . and before you say anything, the day after that it's you-lot time again. *Verte Venise,*' he added mysteriously.

'What on earth's that?'

'It's the canals. Miles of them. With boats, and little islands to picnic on. But first!' He made a fiend's face.

'Churches,' they moaned, but resignedly this time.

'Right.'

'With a good French restaurant lunch in the middle,' said their mother to forestall more groans. 'I've deserved a rest from cooking.'

As always on days when they were going on a parent-choice outing, there was no delay the next morning. There was no need to pack the car or take a picnic, so they were ready to go right after breakfast. The bad thing for Roger was he'd overslept and missed milking; so he set off feeling uncomfortable about not having helped – or seen – Melusine. He particularly wanted to see her this morning, to make sure she was back to her normal, bossy self, but his father was raring to go and in no mood to wait. Anyway Roger didn't want to give the twins anything to send him up about.

It started off as a typically boring Dad-day. He had all the local churches for miles around circled on his tourist map with red marker pen, and to drive the children mad he showed it to them, casually remarking that they were going to do them all. As the map looked as if it had measles, there was marked gloom in the back seat, until their mother reassured them.

'Don't worry, kids. I couldn't take more than four myself without a complete collapse.' The three of them leant over

54

the back of her seat and hugged her thoroughly, while their father said, 'No culture – none of you!'

The first church was quite the dullest Roger had ever seen. To begin with, it was empty, completely empty of everything – no pews (let alone misericords, rude or otherwise) no altar, no tombs (Roger secretly rather liked some tombs, especially the ones with crusaders in armour on them). No brass to rub, no lectern with a bible to let fall open and stab with a finger to read godly messages from, no stained glass, even. All there was were stone walls, crumbling pillars and dusty flag floors. And an echo.

'Woo – woo – aaah!' went Polly ghostlily. And '. . . oooh – aaah . . .' went the echo, much more so, filling the vaulted roofspace with eerie, hollow sound.

The next church, several villages away, was much the same, and they'd got bored with making ghost noises by then.

'Why aren't they being used, Dad?' Roger asked.

'Why are they in such bad repair, is what I'd like to know,' muttered his father. 'I always thought the French were so particular about the upkeep of their historical monuments.'

'I don't see how you could think that, living in our chateau,' said his mother.

'Where are the pews?' asked Emma, who wanted to sit down.

'Maybe people come and steal them,' said Polly.

'You couldn't walk off with a pew, stupid,' said Emma.

'Oh do stop boggering,' hissed Roger in disgust.

'I beg your pardon?' said their father, emerging from his book with his eyebrows well-raised.

The girls giggled. 'It's Woddy for bicker, Dod – I mean Dad,' said Polly. But at least it stopped them. They went out to play pocket Mastermind in the car.

'I'm going too,' said Roger. 'This isn't interesting. It's even emptier than the ballroom in the chateau.'

His father lowered the guide-book and gave him a sharp, interested look.

'Have you seen it then?' he asked.

'Yeah . . . Melusine showed me over the whole place, pretty near.'

'You didn't tell us.' His father sounded exactly like Polly when she thought she'd been left out of something. 'Would she show me the place, do you think?'

'Probably. If you ask her.'

'I'll do that,' his father said decidedly.

They had a marvellous lunch by a river after the third (and, they all devoutly hoped, final) church. There were red checkered tablecloths, tiny crisp circles of French bread with lots of butter (Roger always sprinkled salt on his) and as many delicious thin chips as you wanted with your mini-steak. The waitress came back with refilled baskets of them three times until their dad called a halt. He didn't say no when the manager kept coming back with the large bottle of house wine to refill the grown-ups' glasses, though.

Everyone was happy and rather sleepy after that, but their father was stern and dragged them all off to one last church. It was a longish drive to this one, and all the children dozed off in the back of the car, to be woken by their father exclaiming:

'Ah! Now there's a real humdinger! The guidebook *said* it was something special – wonderful Romanesque carvings!'

The twins wanted to stay in the car, but something different about the building drew Roger out. It wasn't so much a complete church as a ruin with a tower attached. It was the tower that got him: it reminded him of the one at Bois-Serpe, the same size and shape. Except for the carvings.

They were outside, not in – there was nothing inside except bat and bird droppings, and a black look to the walls as if there'd been a fire. But all round the outside, under the eaves of the conical roof, were projections of stone, worn by time and weather, carved into strange and interesting shapes.

Some of them were animals, some flowers, some fanciful designs which weren't exactly like anything Roger could think of. But most of them were people's heads. Some of these were grotesque, gargoyle-looking things with hideous bulbous noses and tongues sticking out. Others looked quite like ordinary people.

'Were these all done by the same person, Dad?'

'I wouldn't say so, would you? They're all different styles.'

They moved slowly round the tower together, gazing upward, calling each other's attention to this head or that.

'There's a funny one – really funny, like a comedian trying to make you laugh by pulling a face.'

'Oh, look at that old woman – she's just like the one in the bread-shop in the village!'

'Yes, some of them are real local types that haven't changed.'

'How old are they, Dad?'

'Eleventh, twelfth century.'

'Wow. Eight hundred years old . . .'

After one circuit of the tower and the ruins, Roger's father sat down on a grassy bank to read his guide book and Roger decided to go round once more. It was on this second trip, when he was by himself, that he saw her.

He stopped dead, staring upwards. How had he missed noticing her the first time? None of the others were like her. For one thing, she wasn't so weather-worn as most of them; her features were still sharp, as if she'd been carved recently. Unlike the others, she was young, almost a child, not an old or at least ageless sort of person. Her hair was parted in the middle and the stone smoothed over its flat planes, and – was there? – yes, there was! – a ridge of stone beside her neck which could be the top of a plait.

But it wasn't just that which made her so familiar to him that it was like looking at a recent portrait. Her round stone eyes, wide mouth, thin face – it was just *her*. It couldn't be, but it was.

And even as Roger stood there gaping up at the little stone head, something even more incredible happened.

His father came strolling round the curve of the tower, his nose still in the guide-book, and said, 'Listen, Rodge, something odd here that'll interest you. Coincidence! I didn't notice before because the church, before it fell down, was called something else. D'you know what this tower is called? It's Tour Melusine.'

8   *The Nightmare*

The trip back was mercifully short, because Roger got car-sick again. This time it was his own fault. No one can read in the back of a car as it goes along without risking being sick. But Roger was so deep in his father's guidebook he didn't notice what was happening to his stomach until it was too late.

This time nobody felt inclined to be nice about it.

After the necessary clean-up, with every window in the car wide open, Roger, feeling guilty, leant back and let his thoughts escape out of the unpleasant present to what he had seen and read.

Melusine was indeed a local name. It was the name of a legendary character, and the tower, and probably several other places, were named after her. Unfortunately Roger had thrown up, and his father had firmly removed the book, before he could find out who the original Melusine had been. But she wasn't – like most people whom church towers are named after – a saint. 'A shadowy mythological figure', the book had said. 'Her origins are lost in the mists of antiquity, but a clue may be found in – ' That was as far as nausea had let him get.

He wanted to get hold of the book the moment they got back to the chateau, but his father took it to read in the loo (a habit of his which Roger's mother deplored). Anyway, it was milking time, so Roger decided to postpone his researches into the ancient Melusine and go and have another look at the modern one.

But when he got to the goat-pen, Melusine wasn't there.

Roger hung around, watching the goats getting more and more restive as their milking time came and went. Like cows, they needed to be milked on time or, it seemed, their udders became too full and started to be uncomfortable. It wasn't like Melusine to leave them to suffer, if that was the word. . . . Roger grew more uneasy and impatient as the animals did. After about three-quarters of an hour he could stand it no longer, and decided to risk a visit to the ogre's kitchen.

He was cautious this time. He crept to the back window as silently as a Red Indian, his sandals making not even a whisper in the rank grasses, and raised his head with infinite slowness to peer in.

At first the habitual darkness of the room made him think it was empty, but then in the furthest corner where he had previously noticed an aged armchair, a little movement suddenly caught his eye.

He swung his head that way. He could scarcely see anything through the dusty window, and what he could see puzzled him so much he blinked several times and screwed up his brows. What he seemed to see was two people sitting in the armchair together, one on the lap of the other.

He ducked his head, and stayed crouched in the grass below the window with his bent knees level with his ears. The seedheads of the long grasses tickled him, and he swiped at a mosquito. He was scowling.

Melusine, sitting on her father's lap?

Well, why not? Polly and Emma often sat on their father's lap, especially around bedtime. At least . . . they used to. Not so much recently. But their father still kissed and hugged them quite often. He kissed Roger, too, from time to time, and their mother, of course, never stopped. They were quite a kissy family; Roger was used to displays of affection.

So why had the sight of Melusine on her father's lap disturbed him?

She had missed the milking. Maybe that was why.

And it was so dark – and – awful in there. What had his mother called the big kitchen?

Squalid.

Dirty. Uncared-for. Repulsive.

Repulsive . . .

Roger repressed a shudder. Yes, he couldn't shake the idea off: there was definitely something repulsive about the scene he had half-witnessed across the stone window-sill.

He decided not to go back to the goat-pen.

So he went home. He looked for the guide-book but not very hard. He went to his own small, clean, unsqualid room after supper and lay on his back reading his *Mad* comic. A lot of it was very funny and he usually cracked up laughing at it, but tonight he just stared at the pages and couldn't even follow the stories. After a while he threw it on the floor and closed his eyes, thinking he must be sleepy.

After a short time he opened them again. The imaginative pictures that had played themselves out behind his eyelids bothered him. He kept seeing the two people in the armchair. There had been movements – like a struggle. He knew it was none of his business and that it was beyond what he was ready to understand. He told himself just to forget about it, but he couldn't.

He lay awake a long time, wondering, not so much what exactly he had seen, but why it had made him feel so upset and angry. In the end the feeling and the bafflement wore him out. He fell into a deep sleep.

In the middle of the night, Roger sat up suddenly in the black darkness.

His face was cold and his hairline prickled. He clenched his fists and pressed them to his stomach. He dared not breathe.

There was some terrible thing in the little room with him. He could hear it whispering. No. Not whispering. Rustling. Very faintly and dangerously rustling across some hard surface – moving towards him.

His brain was blanked out with panic. He couldn't think what he ought to do. He tried to force himself to be calm, to take some evasive action. Turn on the light – no. No, he couldn't, it was by the door and anyway . . . he didn't want to see what it was. He couldn't bear even the idea of seeing what it was.

He felt a heavy, dumb, living weight mount on to the bottom of his bed and lie across his feet.

It pinned his ankles to the mattress. He couldn't move now even if he decided to. It lay there, he felt it, real and substantial through the blanket his mother had thrown over him. It seemed to settle on him, with faint, small, adjusting movements. Images flashed through his half-frozen brain. A cat – no. Too – narrow, too heavy. Too hard. Something – human? Some part of a human being? An arm, that was closer, the heavy, muscled arm of a big man might feel like that. But where was the rest of him?

A mental picture came to him of the only man it could be. Monsieur Serpe. The ogre. Lying on the flag floor in the dark with his arm across Roger's feet. Why? How could he have got in? What did he want? What was he going to do to Roger?

Roger felt something rising in him like vomit, and when it reached his throat he heard himself scream.

It was a fearful sound, more fearful than the fear that had made him let it out. It wrenched him from his paralysis. With a strength he hadn't known he possessed, he dragged his feet out from under the weight, and in the next second he was out of bed and wrestling with the handle of the door.

As he burst through into the kitchen, he came face to face with his father. Roger flung himself into his arms.

The sense of safety was as strong as the fear and almost painfully wonderful. His father held him tightly for a long moment while his inward shuddering and gasping died down. Then he took his arms and held him away a little.

'What's wrong, darling?'

His father seldom called him darling, only at specially

emotional moments. His face was as white as Roger's own. Roger tried to speak and couldn't. He just pointed back into the larder-room.

His father let him go and lurched past him, switching on the light. He hung in the doorway, his head turning as he scanned every inch of the room. Roger just stood there, his arms clutched to his chest; after a moment he felt his mother's arms round him. He was aware of Emma in the background, whimpering with fright. He found himself thinking, 'Polly sleeps through anything,' and when he thought that he knew the worst was over and that he was coming out of his terror.

His father turned back to him.

'There's nothing there, Rodge.'

'It wasn't a dream, Dad.'

'What was it?'

'I heard something. A rustling. I've heard it before in there. And then something – ' He had to stop and swallow, and clear his throat of the horror still lurking there. 'Something came on to the bed. It lay on my feet and I couldn't move.' He was shocked to find his voice wobbling and suddenly he felt a hot lump where the horror had been.

They made a fuss of him, all of them, Emma too. While their mother made cocoa and spoke quietly to their father, Emma comforted him in Woddy.

'Dere wodden noddin in dere, Wodder. Wodder had a dwawful dwoom. Woke Eddy widda noddable scwoom.'

And he was recovered enough to reply, 'Soddy, Eddy. Wodder had a woggable fwot. Wadn't a dwoom. Woddest, id wod weal.' Somehow it was a great help to be able to lapse into this childishness. He only wished that he could tuck into bed with his parents, as he remembered had been the remedy years and years ago when, occasionally, he or the twins would wake up after a nightmare.

But this wasn't a nightmare. He was utterly sure of that. And his father at least believed him, because he said, as he handed Roger his mug of cocoa and put his arm round him, 'Listen, Rodge. There's obviously something about that room that doesn't sit well with you. I think you'd better sleep on the settee in the big room tonight and tomorrow we'll see what we can arrange.'

So they put him to bed on the brocaded sofa next to the beautiful octagonal table with its gem-stone inlays, surrounded by the tapestries and gold-tooled books. He was uneasy because here he was as close as possible to the ogre's kitchen on the other side of the door. But his father sat with him and talked about going to the canals and after a while he felt himself slipping toward sleep. But there was suddenly something he had to know.

'Dad.'

'Yes, Rodge.'

'Did you read in the guidebook about Melusine?'

'Yes, I read all about her. She was quite a character, apparently.'

'Tell me.'

He felt his father's hand on his back, so different from that other pressure, so protective and comforting.

'Not tonight. Now you sleep. I'll stay with you till you do.'

And Roger slept.

9   *Into the Jungle*

Roger woke in the morning with the feeling that someone was watching him.

His eyes snapped open. There *was* someone watching him. It was Melusine. She was standing between the sofa and the window, through which the sun was blazing. Her silhouette was straight and slim, like a column. It cast a shadow right across his face.

Roger, with last night's fear still faintly alive in him, lay for a moment staring at her, wondering if he should feel afraid again. But then he realized that, if he could be wondering that, there was actually nothing to fear.

He sat up on his elbows. '*Bonjour*,' he said.

She didn't answer, but moved slowly towards him and sat down at the foot of the sofa. He jerked his legs out from under her with a gasp of remembered panic. But then he noticed that, with the sun shining on her face, she looked strange, pale through her sunburn and with dark rings under her eyes. She wore her jeans and a clean T-shirt but she smelt of the goats.

'Are you okay?' he asked.

'I am okay. You okay also?'

'Sure. I'm fine. Why are you here?'

She looked down at the quilt that covered him and traced the pattern on it with one grimy finger.

'You go today to Verte Venise?'

'Yeah, if that's the canals.' She looked up at him swiftly. Her expression was beseeching, as he had never seen it – she was begging something from him! On a rash impulse, he heard himself ask: 'You – you want to come?'

She nodded hard.

He had a quick think. This could be tricky.

'Look. You ask your father, and I'll ask mine. The trouble is, there's not really room in the car – but if I sat at the back with the picnic stuff – '

'*Quoi, quoi?*' He was going too fast for her.

He jumped out from under the quilt. 'Don't worry. Just ask – your – father.' When she still looked blank, he tried acting it. In a high squeaky voice, he cried: '"*S'il vous plaît, Papa, puis-je aller avec Roger à les* – er – canals?"' She was watching him, spellbound, which emboldened him. Putting on a gruff and ogre-ish voice, he answered himself: '"*Oui, oui, ma fille, allez!*"'

She burst out laughing. Then she did a funny thing. She clapped both hands over her mouth and seemed to press the laugh back. Her eyes above her hands were wide as if with alarm, and they rested, not on Roger but on the dividing door in the tower wall.

Neither of the fathers, as it turned out, was too keen on the idea, but Roger's father was the sort that tends to say 'no' on principle and then give way, whereas Melusine's father was made of much sterner stuff. Roger's mother had to go round to the side door of the chateau and have a little chat with him in French before he could be persuaded.

'She has to do the milking first,' she reported on her return. 'Go on, Roger, go and help her, then we can get off early.'

'I want to come too,' said Polly unexpectedly as Roger prepared to go out. 'I want to see how she milks the goats.'

'Don't,' he said shortly. 'Not your scene, Poll.' But she tagged along anyhow.

'I want to see how *you* milk them. *If* you really milk them,' she added slyly.

Roger didn't bother answering. He strode ahead of her

66

round the chateau and to the goat pen. He vaulted carelessly over the fence. The goats knew him now and didn't run from him. He began catching them and tethering them in a line. Polly watched, trying not to show she was impressed.

'Aren't you scared they'll butt you?'

'They don't butt me.'

'Can I pat one?'

'Why not?'

She reached over the fence and stroked a floppy ear tentatively.

'You can pull some grass for 'em,' Roger said. 'That's clean work, but mind the nettles.'

To his astonishment she made no objection but did as he said. When he had five goats tied up and Melusine hadn't yet come, he decided to get on with the job on his own. He fetched the pail and stool from the dairy and settled down beside the first goat in the line.

As he grasped the teats, he took a second to savour the deep satisfaction he would get from showing off his new skill for Polly. She was watching him breathlessly . . . He began with strong, slow strokes, sure of his technique. How Poll would gawp at the dring-dring-dring . . .

But there was no dring-dring-dring. There wasn't so much as a plink. Nothing came out, not a drop!

By the time he realized what had happened and stopped wrestling with the empty udder, Polly had finished shrieking with laughter and had skipped away, as nimble and mocking as a goat herself. Roger sat on the stool and pressed his red furious face against the warm smelly flank. He'd have preferred to kick the creature, though it wasn't its fault that Melusine must have done the milking at the crack at dawn, before letting herself into their flat . . . He ground his teeth, listening to the echoes of Polly's laughter.

He got up heavily, put the pail and stool back and released the goats. He felt like leaving them tied up all day just for spite, as if they were the cause of his humiliation. How the twins would send him up! It could easily spoil the whole day.

As he stumped back gloomily past the front of the chateau, he slowed down, as he always did, to glance out at the 'sentries' standing lopsided in their wilderness. And suddenly he thought: *She must have planned it.* Because why else should she get up even earlier than usual to get the milking done? And come to that . . . how did she know that Roger's family were going on an outing? Let alone where to. . . .

He turned and faced the chateau. His eyes wandered to the right toward his family's end of the building. They only occupied the ground floor. He glanced at the windows above their flat, in the wing beyond the tower . . . In one of them were curtains. And, as he looked, one of them moved.

Her bedroom? Right above –

He looked down.

Directly below the curtained window was a little round porthole in the thick stone wall.

His room. . . .

He began to run hard through the grass, his mind working feverishly. Did she have a way to – to listen, to eavesdrop? He was determined to search his room from top to bottom. Perhaps there was even a way for her to get in – a trapdoor, something like that . . . though that was absurd. How could she climb down from the ceiling, why should she want to get in, to scare the daylights out of him? Unless her father. . . .

Because he knew suddenly that he was afraid of that man. Otherwise why should it have been *him* Roger had seen so clearly in his frenzied thoughts last night, the ogre, lying on the floor by his bed with his heavy, muscled arm across Roger's feet . . . ?

But his intention was foiled. Once again there was the car with the hatchback open ready for him to crawl in with the rugs and picnic stuff. The three girls were already in the back seat, his father was locking up the flat. . . .

'Come on, Lonesome Goatherd! If you've *quite* finished

68

milking all your goats!' called Polly through the car window. And she and Emma burst into giggles.

The journey to the canals was fairly hellish for Roger, crouched in the back while the three girls sat with their backs to him, the twins giggling away, ignoring him and his self-sacrificing discomfort (though at least not totally ignoring Melusine. They taught her cat's cradle.) But when they arrived at the canal, everything got better.

At first the place didn't look all that special, just like a canal at home, or a small river, with some houses alongside it, and a boathouse place where you could hire rowing boats. There were too many in their party for one boat, so, after a bit of grumbling, Roger's dad agreed to take two. He and their mother and Emma went in one; Roger, Melusine and Polly in the other.

'Can you row?' Roger's father asked Melusine, showing by gestures what he meant.

She shook her head.

'Can you swim?' he asked, swimming in the air. Melusine shrugged rather guardedly.

'Never mind, Brian. They all have to wear life jackets. And they won't do anything silly, will you, darlings?'

' "Better drowned than duffers, if not duffers won't drown", eh?' said their father heartily. Roger and the girls looked blank.

'Arthur Ransome. *Swallows and Amazons*. Oh, hell, what can you do with kids who don't read? Go on then, but be careful.'

There was a lot of scrambling in, and shrieks as the boats rocked, and cautious handing over of picnic things. Only Melusine kept quiet and preserved her dignity, stepping lightly into the boat and sitting in the stern with her hands (now spotless) clasped between her knees and her back ramrod straight.

Roger insisted that his boat have its share of picnic items, in case they got separated.

'But you're not to get separated!' his mother said sharply. 'You're to keep right behind us!' Roger and Polly, their earlier enmity forgotten, exchanged quick, complicitous looks.

'Woo'll soo about dot,' muttered Polly. 'Dead bordin, fodderin, eh, Wodder?'

'Wight, Pod. Lod's tog off od our wone.'

'Stop talking Woddy at once, what are you plotting, you little villains?' called their mother.

'Nothing, Mum!' they called back innocently.

'You'd better not be,' she said darkly, while Emma, who'd opted for the parental boat because her father was the fastest and best rower, suddenly realized she might have made a ghastly mistake. Across the green canal water she sent a mad cross-eyed look which said, 'Don't you dare do anything without me!'

The boat man cast off the lines and their journey along the canal began.

Roger faced backwards and rowed the first stint. Polly was actually a better rower than he was, but she'd draped herself in the prow of the boat trailing her limp hand in the water. She was evidently pretending to be some picture-hatted heroine in a romantic movie, though the bulky life jacket didn't help.

As he rowed steadily along in his father's wake, Roger couldn't help watching Melusine – she was straight ahead of him. *She* was not draped, or pretending to be anything. She sat still as a statue, very upright and almost prim in her green trousers and blouse, with a brown jacket over it. Her hair was pulled straight back so that you could see her head-shape outlined cleanly, not like the twins whose heads were always cluttered with curls.

She was not looking around at the view, or at the water, or at anything but straight back at Roger. Her black button eyes were fixed on him unwinkingly. Her mouth, which had always seemed so straight and thin-lipped, was softer now, loosely closed as if it might smile. He tried a smile on her, and it worked. She smiled back, but twitchily, as if she hadn't meant to.

Roger thought he had been staring at her too long.

'It's nice here, isn't it,' he said – and only then glanced around to see if it really was.

They'd already left the buildings behind and were sliding along under an endless arch of tall, old trees. Their lacy leaves cast shadow-patterns on the greenish canal and across Melusine's face. There were no human noises, other than the splash of the oars; just birdsong and insect song. The air was hot and heavy with moisture. The banks were wild and unkempt. If the canal hadn't been so straight, so obviously man-made, it would have felt a lot like a jungle.

He said that. 'It's like a jungle. Like Africa, or South America.'

'It's not hot enough,' put in Polly from behind him. 'And there'd be monkeys going wow-wow-wow in the trees.'

'They don't go wow-wow-wow,' said Roger irritably. 'Do you think monkeys talk Woddy?' He wished Polly would vanish. Instead, she undraped and said in an undertone, 'There's a lovely little turning just ahead.'

Roger looked over his shoulder and saw it – a branch canal, on their right.

'If Dad turns down there,' muttered Polly, not bothering with Woddy because they were far enough behind the other boat, 'we could go straight on.'

'Or if he doesn't, we could turn,' said Roger.

'Better let them get a bit more ahead. Then we can always say we didn't see which way they went.'

Roger slowed his stroke, winking at Melusine, who looked alert but uncomprehending. After a minute or two, Polly said, 'He's turning!'

Again Roger looked. Sure enough, the other boat turned at right angles. Their mother pointed the way with big gestures. Furthermore she kept her head turned to make sure they were following.

'Dwot and dwoddle!' muttered Polly, giving vent to a Woddy curse. 'We can't.'

However, about a hundred yards further along, the branch canal curved. The other boat passed out of sight around the grassy bank – and just there, almost lost in the undergrowth, they saw yet another, smaller branch-off – a narrow canal stretching away enticingly into the forest.

'Turn, Rodge, quick!' hissed Polly. 'We can be out of sight before they notice we've gone!'

Without hesitation Roger pulled on the right-hand oar, trailing the other in the water. The nose of the boat came round. He pulled strongly with both arms, a thrill going through him as he imagined that they had to escape some fell pursuers. In a few moments the low branches and overhanging bushes had hidden them, and they were heading down a low, green tunnel into unknown waters.

10   *Under the Surface*

At first Roger simply felt keyed-up by that irresistible
excitement that comes of evading one's parents, of
striking out on one's own, breaking rules, having a bit of an
adventure. There'd be some bother at the end of it, no doubt
– a telling-off, some shouting, perhaps a minor punishment.
Well worth it, obviously, for this. . . .

The first thing Polly did to celebrate was to remove her life-
jacket. Roger felt her moving about in the front of the boat,
and, looking over his shoulder, saw her lifting the thing over
her head.

At once, the thrilling sense of freedom thinned as he heard
himself say: 'Don't, Poll. You have to keep that on.'

She threw him a look of scorn.

'What do you think I'm going to do, jump out and drown?'

'You never know.'

'Don't be so boring.'

'Well, I'm not going in after you.'

'Who needs you to? Anyway I can swim better than you.'

Roger turned to face Melusine again. She had made a
sound to attract his attention. She was looking alarmed.

'Where we are go? Why not to go with you parents?'

'We're escaping,' he said with a grin. '*Échapper.*'

'But why?' He shrugged humorously. She dropped her
voice and leaned forward. 'You not like your father, that you
échappe from him?'

Startled, Roger said: 'Dad's all right. We're just having a
bit of fun, that's all.'

73

She made tutting noises like a grown-up. '*Tu es méchant!*' she said in a scolding tone.

'Oh, so what? You can't be good all the time!' he said irritably. She was spoiling it, the excited feeling, dragging him back to ordinariness and rules. Really, Melusine was strange, she was almost like a grown-up at times. For a minute Roger wished Emma was sitting there in the stern instead.

They rowed on for some time in silence. The birds were not so noisy here; they seemed to prefer the main channels where more light came through the trees. Here it was deeply shady, quiet – remote. It was easy to feel that there were no houses or people for miles.

They glided toward a huge tree which had been torn up by the roots, perhaps by a storm. It lay at an angle across the canal, its branches propped up by trees on the opposite bank; but it was the rooty part that held their gaze – a huge, round clod of earth almost as big as the front of a house, with the roots sticking out at the back. They all turned their heads to look at the felled forest giant, and Roger dragged the oars in the water to bring the boat to a stop beneath it. It reminded him somehow of the gateposts near the chateau . . . Polly from behind him suddenly said:

'Everglades.'

'What?'

'It's a place. I've seen it in films. It's like this. Miles and miles of water and trees . . . with big roots. And snakes. And crocodiles. Prisoners escaping from chain-gangs steal boats and get lost there, and if they fall out the crocodiles eat them. Look! There's even the same spooky mist rising from the water.'

She was right. The heat under the canopy of low-hanging trees was now so heavy that it drew a steam from the solid-looking green surface, as if from a witch's cauldron just gone off the boil.

Suddenly a bird gave voice. Not a chirp or a twitter. A

harsh, jungly cry, from one of the deep thickets on either side. Polly jumped, rocking the boat.

'What was that?' Polly gasped.

'Nothing, just a bird. Stop jumping about, will you?'

'It's scary in here!' She shook herself, then said briskly: 'Come on, it's my turn to row.'

'We can't change places here. I'll pull in to the bank.' He laid hold of the oars and prepared to turn.

'There's nowhere proper to land. It's okay, I'll just – '

She stood up, just as he started to turn toward the bank – hit her head on the half-fallen tree – and fell straight out of the boat.

The clonk of her head hitting the wood, the leap of the boat as she left it, and the loud splash, caused Roger to drop the oars and spin round. She hadn't screamed. She vanished into the scummy water and it closed over her without sound.

'Poll! Polly!' he bellowed, more in fury than fright at first. Then, when nothing happened, his voice rose to a squeak of terror. '*Polly!*'

Silence. The bird cried again as if in mockery: *Told you so! Told you so!* Roger's wits completely deserted him. It had happened so quickly! He half stood, half crouched there in the rocking boat, expecting her head to break the surface, expecting – expecting it not to have happened.

But it had. She was gone.

He must jump in after her. He must. He dropped again on to the seat, his eyes fastened to the spot where his sister had vanished, kicking at the heels of his trainers, but they came right up over his ankles, you couldn't kick them off without unlacing them . . . Well, straight in, then – He stood up, preparing to jump, his mind a rigorous blank, *do it, don't think about it, do it –*

Suddenly the boat leapt again. Instinctively he clutched the gunwales to steady himself, and looked toward the stern.

Melusine was gone.

He saw only the swirl in the green water beside where she

had been seated. And something – a blackish undulating line – her pigtail? – it must be! – wriggled, swished audibly through the turbulence and submerged.

Jumped? – but why? Fallen? – but how?

Again, desperately, he prepared to jump in. But something stopped him. There was some underwater upheaval occurring just below the boat that upset his balance and made him crouch down again instinctively. Something big was threshing about down there. The little rowboat rose and fell as if the canal was drawing deep, gasping breaths beneath it.

Roger was paralysed with shock, with fear. He could think of only one thing, sitting there clinging to the oarlocks with white knuckles.

A crocodile . . . impossible! And yet . . .

A moment of utter silence and stillness, of darkness in Roger's mind.

Then suddenly there was a bubbling burst of sound. He opened his eyes and ricked his neck turning toward it. Polly's head had shot out of the water as if propelled from below. Her face was ghastly, deathly white under streaks of glistening mud, her hair plastered to her skull. Her eyes were closed, but her mouth dropped open the second it was clear of the water.

As Roger reached out and grabbed any bit of her he could get hold of – round her neck with one hand, under her armpit with the other – he felt her body being shoved higher by something unseen in the depths. This – force – whatever it was, thrust her right up out of the water to her waist, so that, with him pulling, she fell half-way into the boat. After that it was comparatively easy for him to drag her the rest of the way, though the boat nearly capsized before he managed to balance it with his own weight.

She lay in the bottom, streams of water pouring from her hair, her clothes. He threw himself on to her back with all his strength, and more water gushed out of her mouth and nose. He lifted himself, then fell on her again. More water was expelled. As he came off her a second time, she gave a retching cough, and then he heard a great noisy gasp of air rush into her lungs. It was the most marvellous, the most relieving sound he had ever heard in his life.

He leant back, sweat breaking out all over him as he looked down at her. She was breathing now, snoringly. She would be all right! He wondered if he should lug her upright or leave her lying on her front. He decided to lift her a bit, and as he was struggling to do this he suddenly let her go again.

Melusine . . .!

He looked round wildly. And at once he saw her! He felt all the blood leave his face.

She was crouching in the stern of the boat, just behind him. Her face was pale, exhausted even, but composed. She gave him a little glance in which concern and reassurance were somehow mixed, and insinuated herself gently into his place.

She raised Polly's middle and pushed her abandoned life-jacket under her waist, so that the top half of her body sloped downwards. Then she indicated that Roger should give her his life-jacket. With half-numb fingers he undid the straps and pulled it over his head. He felt the cold on his back and chest where he had been sweating.

Melusine took a handful of his shirt and showed him she wanted that, too. He peeled it off. She carefully, even tenderly dried Polly's face with it, then folded it and put it under her head so that she had a sort of flat pillow. She then took off her own life-jacket, and after it the jacket she was wearing. She spread this lengthways over Polly to warm her.

Roger crouched there, unable to move. His eyes were riveted to the jacket.

It was perfectly dry.

He looked incredulously at Melusine, still tending Polly, murmuring to her now, rubbing her hands and slapping them to wake her up. Roger reached out his own hand and secretly touched the leg of Melusine's trousers.

They were dry. *She was dry all over.* Her pigtail, that he had distinctly seen vanishing into the canal, was dry. She had not a drop of water on her.

He couldn't believe it. He could not believe it.

Then he thought of something else. She'd been wearing her life-jacket. You couldn't dive underwater with a life-jacket on. He'd tried it once. You couldn't.

She turned to him, met his eyes – her round black ones were perfectly calm. She put her fists in front of her and demonstrated rowing, then pointed at him, then back the way they had come.

'We go now. You parents.'

Like a clockwork toy that's been wound up, he seated himself and took up the oars. Melusine stayed in the front with Polly, who was now stirring and muttering and coughing. Roger was facing the other way, toward the stern. He began to row – that was what the clockwork toy had been programmed to do. That was how he felt. He was just glad he was able to do *something*.

He rowed back through the tree-tunnel. Numb.

At the far end, near where they had turned off, he heard voices. He knew it was his parents – soon he could distinguish his father's voice, then his mother's, then Emma's, calling their names: 'Polly! Roger! Melusine! Where are you?' They sounded frantic.

He felt the beginnings of an awful shame.

As they came out into the secondary canal and began to glide toward the sound of the cries, he felt Melusine's hand on his shoulder. Using him as a fulcrum she levered herself over the oar, a leg at a time. He watched her slide down to her original place at the back of the boat and seat herself neatly, precisely, as before, back straight, head up, hands clasped between her knees. It was as if she were distancing herself from what had happened. Which was fair, thought Roger despairingly – it had been nothing to do with her.

Only by the fact that she was wearing her blouse and not

her jacket could you tell that all was not just as it had been when they started.

Had she been in the water or hadn't she?

He shook his head so violently he ricked his neck again. He must be going mad, that was all. He must be going mad. Or else it was the shock. Yes, that was it. He'd imagined a crocodile. He must have imagined . . . All of it?

He glanced round. Polly lay on her front with her behind sticking up, her eyes a quarter open, groaning and catching her breath, wet, soaked, sodden . . . That horror was real enough.

He hadn't imagined her shooting up to the surface when she was unconscious. That had happened. If it hadn't . . .

Looking at Melusine, seated there so dry and so – so controlled, he felt a shudder run over him from head to foot. In the blazing noon heat he turned as cold as ice.

11   *The Lopsided Gatepost*

'You ought to have jumped in. Without hesitating or
shilly-shallying. It should have been *automatic*.'

It was evening. Polly had been seen by a local doctor, who
had wanted to take her to hospital in Niort, the nearest large
town thirty miles away, but in the end he'd agreed that her
mother could nurse her at home. He bandaged the bump on
her head and said severely that she'd had a very narrow
escape from drowning. When he said this, he scowled at her
parents in a way that made them both hang their heads like
guilty children.

It was while they were having a scratch supper (it was the
uneaten picnic) in the kitchen later, that Roger's father, after
a long silence, suddenly burst out with his accusation against
Roger.

Roger didn't even try to answer. He'd been saying the same
thing to himself ever since the accident happened. His father's
words – and the still-white faces of both his parents – were
the last straw. He jumped up from his untouched meal and
ran into his bedroom where he shut the door and slumped on
to the narrow bed. His misery was too deep for any display of
it. He just sat there.

He could hear his father and mother arguing in the kitchen
in low, tense voices. Occasionally he could make out a bit of
what they were saying.

'. . . want him to risk . . . drowned too? . . .'
'. . . his fault in the first place . . . going off like . . .'
'. . . make him feel worse than . . . already . . .'

80

'. . . be more responsible . . . sister . . .'

'. . . started . . . bit of naughtiness – only a kid . . .'

'. . . our fault too, I suppose . . .'

'. . . poor kid . . . go and – '

There was the scrape of a chair. Roger tensed. His father was going to come in now and try to take back his harsh words. Roger's eyes went to the door almost fearfully, wishing he could lock it, lock his father out, lock everybody out. He wanted to just stay in there by himself until he could calm down, work things out. The only person he could bear the idea of being with was . . . his mind paused on this thought. He'd started it with the idea of Emma, but suddenly he realized it was Melusine's face that came into his mind.

Anyway, his father did come in, sat down beside him, put an arm round him, said he was sorry, it had just burst out, nobody could blame Roger really, he himself didn't know how he would have behaved in such a moment. Nobody knew till it happened to them. It was just that. . . . And here his father started to ramble, explaining why he'd said what he had, how there was this feeling that a chap should just do the right and brave thing instinctively, but lots of chaps didn't, it wasn't their fault . . . and on and on till Roger couldn't stand it a second longer.

'Shut up, Dad!' he burst out loudly.

His father stopped talking at once, patted him on the shoulder, kissed the side of his head, and went out of the room, closing the door softly.

Roger sat on. It was good to be alone, he wanted to be, yet when there was a tap on the door some time later and Emma whispered, 'Can I come in, Rodge?' he was relieved.

'How is she?' he asked at once.

'She's okay. She's asleep. Don't worry, she'll be great tomorrow.'

'Are you sure?'

'Yes, the doctor said.'

She sat where their father had sat. After a while, she said: 'I don't understand how you saved her if you didn't jump in.'

It had been difficult to explain this part of the story. The grown-ups had brushed over it, evidently supposing that Polly had not actually submerged and that Roger had heaved her back into the boat by himself somehow. All they cared about was that she was rescued. But Emma was not so easily satisfied.

'Look,' he said, 'I don't know how to explain it. She sank. She'd gone. Then suddenly she – kind of – shot out of the water, as if – ' He paused. She was gazing at him. He swallowed, and then said: 'You know that awful bit in *Jaws II* when the shark got that boy, and kind of lifted him up and slammed him right into the side of the sailboat? Like, he was dead, and the shark – '

Emma shuddered and nodded. The image had haunted them all for weeks, though they had pretended to joke about it.

'It was a bit – like that. Something – pushed her – half-way out of the water.'

'What was it? How could it?'

He shrugged, not looking at her.

'Maybe she pushed herself up from the bottom.'

'No. She was unconscious. She couldn't.'

'Then – '

He turned to face her.

'Em, I think . . . I think it may have been Melusine.'

'*Melusine?*'

'I know. She didn't look as if she'd been in the water. But she had. She went in. I felt the boat get lighter. I looked around and she'd gone.' He paused, frowning. A splash? Had he heard a splash? He couldn't remember one, but there must have been. 'And then,' he went on, 'there was a great – I don't know – something twisting and heaving under the boat – and up she came, Poll, I mean, like – she just shot up, as if something got hold of her legs and just – shoved her out of the water.'

'I don't get it.'

'Me neither. It was really weird.'

'And then what happened? How did Melusine get back in the boat?'

'I don't know. Suddenly she was there. She – she was dry. I don't know. It made me feel all funny, as if. . . .' He didn't finish.

After a while Emma said, 'I think there's something strange about her altogether.'

He turned to her quickly.

'What do you mean?'

'She's weird, that's all. I can't explain. When we were showing her cat's cradle, she'd obviously never done it before, but she learnt it at once. Her fingers . . . Have you ever touched her hands?'

'W – well . . . sort of . . . while we were milking.'

'Didn't you notice how sort of *funny* they are?'

'You mean – cold?'

'Not exactly. Just – different. And then there's the way she moves.'

'How?'

'She doesn't walk. She glides.' Roger felt a jerk of recognition in his head. He stared at her. 'And her eyes. Her eyes are so – '

Suddenly he gripped her wrist to silence her.

They both heard it. It was a faint sound overhead – a footfall. They looked up at the ceiling. Another! Someone was moving about in the room above.

'It's her room,' whispered Roger.

'Are you sure – ?'

'No, but I think so.'

'Can she hear us?' Emma mouthed without sound.

Roger remembered how, this morning (only this morning!)

Melusine had known where they were going. He mouthed back, 'Maybe.'

Emma rose, and beckoned. Together they tiptoed out of the room, into the kitchen, and out of the chateau by the kitchen French windows.

It was already dusk. They walked about twenty paces down the 'garden' and turned to look back. Above their flat with its lights ablaze, was a window with a fainter light. Some skimpy curtains were drawn but they could see the light glowing through.

'That's not a proper electric light,' said Emma.

'I don't think they have electricity at all in their part,' said Roger. 'It must be an oil lamp. It's too bright to be a candle.'

'That's dangerous . . . It must be awful to be so poor, and have to have rich people to stay in your house.'

'Who's rich? We're not rich!'

'I mean, compared to them. Compared to them, we're rolling.'

They stood for a while as dusk fell, gazing at the bulk of the chateau. It was changing from gold to grey and would soon go black.

'I'd love to explore it,' said Emma.

'Would you?' asked Roger, surprised. He didn't think Emma was the exploring type. Then he thought, 'She's only saying that to please me,' the way he sometimes pretended interest in something his father was keen on so as to feel closer to him. He was touched that Emma would bother, but then, she did have this good side, that she occasionally sympathized with him when he was feeling down . . .

'Listen, I'll show you one thing if you like. Come on, before all the light goes.'

He led her over the wall and along the track. The sky was still red in the west; the sun had only just gone down beyond the river-line of the willows. The glow made the sentry gateposts into silhouettes, one lopsided.

Roger stopped in line with the great double front doors and pointed out across the field toward the sunset.

'See? Those were the original gateposts. There was a massive drive here once, and probably a high wall or a railing. Right around the whole chateau. And its grounds. Must've been huge gardens and stuff in those days.'

Emma stared. 'So?'

'Well . . . I mean, it gives you an idea of how grand the place must have been in its – you know, heyday. You can imagine carriages turning in there and coming straight up to the door, and servants coming down the steps to help people out. Like in a film.'

'We've seen much grander houses at home – stately homes. Still being lived in.'

'Yeah, of course. The point is – ' He stopped. She was yawning. 'The *point* is,' he went on doggedly, 'not that this is grand now, but that it isn't.'

'Huh?'

Roger sighed. This was not working.

'It makes it all much creepier, and more interesting, that's all. Anyhow, I think it does.'

'Well, I don't,' said Emma briskly. She could get brisk exactly like Polly at times, usually when she was feeling uneasy. 'I think it's pathetic. I don't want to think about it. I hate this place, if you want to know, I wish we'd gone back to Newport this year. At least we had a proper bath there . . . Come on, we'd better get back or we'll be stepping in goat-muck again in the dark.'

And she ran off without looking back.

Roger started to follow her, and then stopped. He watched her running through the dwindling light, back toward the shining welcome of their French windows. He glanced up. The dimmer glow behind the flimsy curtains in Melusine's room (if it was) had gone out. . . . Did she go to bed so early? Was she, like himself, feeling hollow and a bit sick and incredibly tired after the day's events?

Tomorrow at milking time he would ask her, ask her properly, make her tell him what had really happened in the boat. . . . He shrank from the idea, but he knew he must. He would never be able to stop thinking about it, otherwise, and while he thought about it he would never stop feeling guilty.

He wondered uneasily whether she had told her father. About the danger she had been in, that Roger had let her be in. . . . If the old man took a shot at him now, nobody could blame him.

He found himself turning away from the dark bulk of the building and walking slowly out along the overgrown drive toward the gateposts. They seemed to draw him somehow, as if they were actually people standing out there alone and wanting company. He knew it was silly. He knew it was he who was lonely and that two huge blocks of stone wouldn't be much help. . . .

Still, he walked on, feeling the tug and tap of the grasses and weeds on his legs, listening to the frog-chorus which had just started up from the river, keeping his eyes fixed on the more lopsided of the two square pillars.

Soon he stood between them. They dwarfed him. Each one was twice as tall as himself. He walked to the leaning one and ran his hand over its flat side. The stone seemed to have drunk the day's heat and now gave it back. He felt comforted in the shadow of this huge old block, which loomed over him, like a friendly giant bending down to hear what he said.

'Stand up straight,' Roger muttered to it. 'You're not finished yet.' For no special reason, he put his shoulder against it and gave it a mighty shove.

It moved.

Fractionally – but it moved. He even heard it move, a raw grinding sound from its base.

He jumped back.

There was a second's stillness, then it tilted several inches further toward its fellow.

86

It was now poised at an angle so acute that it seemed impossible it should not fall the rest of the way to the ground. Roger dared not move for fear the least vibration should tip the balance. Nothing more happened, though he waited for what seemed like ages. Finally, cautiously, he backed off.

The last of the daylight was leaving the western sky. The silhouettes were hardly discernible. But the angle – ! It couldn't stand long like that. Roger thought of the great tree they had seen, torn up by its roots. A strong wind, in this exposed spot, and – crash! That'd be the end of the gatepost.

And he'd have helped.

He heaved a deep sigh. Not his day. Couldn't seem to do anything without it going wrong. And now he had to go back and sleep in that scary larder. Emma would have the big room, because the doctor had said their mother should sleep with Polly. And though his father had been sympathetic last night, he was hardly in a mood tonight to listen to Roger's 'bogey-man' fears, quite unproved – he'd be told to be sensible. Well, he'd have to cope with it somehow, and after the terrors of today he began to wonder if, after all, he *had* dreamt last night's intrusion. . . .

He stuffed his cold hands into his pockets and tramped back.

12   *Revelation in a Storm*

B ut it turned out differently.
His father not only hadn't forgotten about last night,
he had no intention of making Roger sleep in that room again
if he didn't want to. At his father's suggestion, Roger was to
sleep with him in the double bed.

Roger, who had been sitting on his fear because he thought
he had no alternative, suddenly felt light-headed with hunger.
He went to the little fridge where he found the remains of the
sandwiches wrapped in foil and ate four of them. Still
munching the last one, he went to have a peep at Polly.

She was awake. He climbed the two steps to her bed and
sat down on it.

'Hi, Poll,' he said. 'You okay?'

'I feel all right. Better, anyhow,' she said. 'But I keep
thinking about it happening. Like film in a loop, over and
over.'

'Poor ode Pod,' he said, using Woddy to express his
sympathy.

'It was my own fault,' she said. 'Standing up like that.
Really stupid. Right out of order.'

'Dad said I should've gone straight in after you,' said
Roger.

'Why should you have? You said you wouldn't, when I
took my life jacket off.'

'I – ' Roger stopped. 'Listen, Poll. Do you – I mean, can
you remember anything that – happened to you, when you
were, you know, under the water? I mean . . . did you feel
anything? How did you come to the surface, for instance?'

Polly looked blank. 'How could I feel anything? I was conked out. Anyway, it's okay now. Don't worry about it. But it was *well* horrid when I came to. I thought I was choking to death . . . Pod wooden dike to dwown, Wodder.'

'Oh, shooting's the best way to die,' he remarked seriously. 'Obviously. Much the quickest.'

'Thanks, I'll try to remember next time,' she said sarcastically, so then he felt she really was better.

He was sent to bed early, and though he made the ritual objections he wasn't really sorry. It was lovely to climb into the big bed and know that he wouldn't be alone there all night. He dozed fitfully till his father came to bed, not all that much later. He moved closer to him and his father gave him a cuddle, just like when he was young.

'Do you feel a bit shaky about it all still? I know I do.'

'Yeah. A bit.'

They lay quietly in the semi-darkness.

'Dad.'

'H'm?'

'What d'you think of Monsieur Serpe?'

'Not a lot.'

'Why?'

After a pause, his father said, 'Dunno, really. Just took against the man as soon as I saw him. "I do not like thee, Dr Fell, the reason why I cannot tell, but this I know, and know right well: I do not like thee, Dr Fell." '

'D'you think he's bad?'

'Bad how?'

'I mean – d'you think . . . do you think he's nice to Melusine?'

'Why? Have you seen signs that he isn't?'

Roger was silent.

'Dad,' he said after a bit.

'H'm?'

'Is it okay for a father to – well, to kiss his daughter, and – you know, sit with her on his knee?'

'Why ever not?'

'I don't know – I just wondered. . . .'

'Does he do that?'

'I saw him. Through the window. He was sitting with her on his lap, kissing her, and she. . . . Well. She didn't look as if she liked it.'

His father lay quiet for a while. Then he gave a little grunt.

'It's not really our business, Roger,' he said. 'Still . . . I won't pretend I like the sound of that very much.'

'Why?'

His father sighed.

'Well. Let me put it like this. A man who lives without a wife, like Monsieur Serpe, can get very lonely. Especially in a remote place like this, with no adult company. And if he's got a young daughter, sometimes he can get – a bit fonder of her than he ought to.'

Roger sat up.

'You mean – like on TV – you mean child abuse?'

'Lie down, son. I'm definitely not saying it's that.'

'But that's with strangers, not a person's father!'

After a longish silence, his father said, 'Nobody likes to tell kids this, but I'm afraid it happens a lot inside families as well. Especially between fathers and daughters.'

Roger was still sitting up, every muscle tense, like last night when he was alone and afraid.

'But that's really wrong,' he said in a low voice.

'Well, yes, it would be, if – if it were that. But we mustn't jump to conclusions, Rodge. Perhaps he was just, you know, making a fuss of her like any father might.' But even as he said it, his voice petered out. The idea of the ogre as 'just like any father' struck even him as doubtful.

'But she was struggling!' said Roger.

'Are you absolutely sure about that?'

Roger was silent. It had been so dark in there. He might easily have misinterpreted the movements he saw in the armchair.

90

'One has to be so terribly careful about accusing people, even in one's own mind,' his father said. But it was clear to Roger that he was troubled. 'Now go to sleep. It's been quite a day. And I don't want you getting hot and bothered about this other business because we really can't get involved.'

'Why not?'

After another pause, his father said, 'Because in just over a week, we'll be going home.'

'You mean, if something bad is going on, we just have to go away and – leave her?'

'Be reasonable, son. What can we do?'

'Take her with us!' burst out Roger, but he knew that was nonsense even before his father said gently, 'Oh, come on, now.'

In the middle of the night Roger woke up to find his face was wet.

The water on his face was cold, and – as he lay there, another drop fell right in his eye with a splash.

'Dad!' he cried, sitting up. 'Wake up!'

His father leapt out of sleep and out of the bed in one bound.

'What! What is it!'

'I think the roof's leaking – my pillow's all wet!'

His father blundered to the door and tried to switch the light on but nothing happened. He swore. 'The power's off!' He paused. 'Listen to that wind!'

As he spoke a deep rumble of thunder sounded, not quite overhead, and a few seconds later came the lightning. Now they listened, they could hear the rain beating on the windows, and the wind certainly was clamouring under the eaves.

'How can the rain get in here, Dad? It's not the top floor,' said Roger from his wet bed.

'God knows, maybe the room upstairs is unoccupied and

the rain's coming through the roof and through the floor up there . . .' He uttered another curse as he stubbed his toe on something. 'I'm going to find the torch.'

'I know where it is!' said Roger, somewhat guiltily jumping up and feeling his way toward the door. He had nicked it some days ago to keep in his larder-room as insurance against night frights.

'Be quiet as you go through the girls' room,' said his father. 'Don't wake Polly.'

Roger tiptoed into the room where Polly and his mother lay sleeping. But his mother wasn't fully asleep and sat up.

'What's going on?' she whispered.

'It's the storm. Your bedroom's sprung a leak.'

'Oh, no! Are we to be spared nothing?' she asked, exasperated. At this moment Emma's little figure appeared.

'I can't get my light to light,' she said in a small voice. She wasn't too keen on storms, especially the thunder. 'I woke up in the big room and I didn't know where I was, at first.'

'It's okay, don't panic,' said their father testily. 'It's just a damned bore, that's all. I saw some candles somewhere. Come on, Rodge, show me where that torch has got to.' And he went through into the kitchen, taking Roger with him.

'Now where is it?'

'It's in my room, Dad.'

'Okay, go and get it. God, what a night!' he exclaimed, as a gust of savage wind made the French windows rattle. 'Talk about extremes of climate!'

Roger felt his way in almost total darkness into his little cell, pushing his feet slowly across the flags, groping his way bedward. The torch was under his pillow. His hands found the edge of the bed and reached for where the pillow should have been.

Instead he touched Melusine's arm.

He was so sure it was her that he wasn't afraid, just astounded. What on earth was she doing in his bed . . . ?

'Melusine . . . ?' he whispered incredulously – and moved

his hand along her arm, that special, warm-cool, hard-soft skin he had touched before which could only be hers.

But it wasn't. Because the arm went on and on and wasn't an arm at all.

It wasn't skin, either. A couple of seconds of touching it told him it wasn't skin. He didn't know what it was, but it was nothing human, though it quivered with life. As his hand followed the wholly un-arm-like curve of the thing on the bed, it moved. It moved! And at the same moment a flash of lightning through the little round window illuminated, just for a split second, what lay under his hand.

But he didn't need the shock of seeing it. He had already realized, in a mental flash more blinding than any lightning, that what he was touching was not skin but scales. Not a girl's arm, or a man's, but the long, firm body of a huge snake.

13   Terror and Calm

He snatched away his hand and backed in the darkness till he hit the back of his head on the shelf across the wall above the porthole window. His body blocked this, preventing any light at all getting into the room.

He stood there for a timeless period, his mind at war with itself.

It couldn't be, but it was. He had felt it and seen it.

Why wasn't he screaming? Why wasn't he running?

Instead of doing either, he said in a low, tense voice, 'Go away. You must go away. *Quickly*.'

And it went. He heard it. He knew the sound of its movement by now, that whispering, rustling sound, the tissue-paper sound. He could follow it without seeing it – it came off the bed on to the flag floor, away into the far corner, and then – where? Up the wall. Yes. He could hear it moving up the powdery plaster wall, having some difficulty in getting a grip, slipping once, then making it to the ceiling, or somewhere. He heard it drag its scaly body out of his room through some aperture which he had planned, out in the field yesterday, to search for. The hole through which Melusine listened or watched him from her bedroom above.

In a state of calm which amazed him, he reached for the torch, found it and walked out, back into the kitchen where his father had now found the candles by touch and lit one.

'What the hell took you so long? Couldn't you find it?'

'Here,' said Roger, hearing his voice come out normally, and noticing, as if it belonged to someone else, that his hand was quite steady. His father, irritable now, almost snatched the torch from him.

'I'm going to take some saucepans and things into the bedroom to catch the drips,' he said shortly. 'You light more candles and put them around the place so your sisters won't be scared.' He went out.

Roger did as he was told. He was not thinking or feeling. It was as if he were watching someone else behaving in an unbelievably controlled way. His hands functioned automatically, lighting the candles, warming the bases of them and sticking them into saucers and ashtrays he found. His mother came in and helped, not noticing anything strange about him. But then there was nothing to notice.

She put Emma to bed in her own bed in the girls' room. Roger followed with a lighted candle. Their mother bent over Polly to tuck her in – somehow she hadn't woken up.

A loud clap of thunder almost right overhead startled his mother, and she clutched Roger's hand for a moment. Emma whimpered. 'Mum! I'm scared . . .'

'Nonsense, darling, it's only a storm. Just thank heaven your ceiling isn't leaking! Now get to sleep.'

She kissed her and pushed Roger ahead of her back into the kitchen. Roger could feel a slight trembling in her hand as it touched his shoulder.

'Leave the door open!' Emma called after them.

Roger's mother left the door ajar and sat down at the table. Lightning lit up the room, and for that second the candles were nothing but painted orange flame-shapes giving no light at all. Roger sat opposite his mother.

'I must say I think it's too bad,' she said in a shrill whisper. 'We're paying the earth for this place! It's all very well, all the glamour, but first they might have made sure it's watertight.'

Roger heard his own voice say levelly, 'It's okay, Mum. Dad'll take care of it.'

'Yes, but where are we going to sleep?' said his mother in

the same shrill tone, quite unlike her normal voice. And suddenly Roger saw that she was on the point of tears.

He got up and stood next to her and put his arm round her shoulders. It was most unusual for her to cry, but he was not surprised nor embarrassed. She had had a bad day and now she'd been woken up and the storm had upset her, and she had nowhere to sleep.

'Why don't you go in and sleep on the settee in the big room?'

She looked up at him. Her face was pale and strained in the candlelight. 'But where will you sleep?'

'I'll sleep in my own room,' he said. The words surprised him no less than the fact that his voice unexpectedly cracked down into a deeper register. His mother's strained face burst into a smile.

'Roger! Did you hear that? Your voice has started to break!'

'Yeah, I heard.' *I'll sleep in my own room.* Was he mad? But he didn't want to take his words back.

His father came in and said he'd moved the bed to a place where the floor seemed dry and with a bit of juggling with the bedclothes at least one person could sleep in it. Maybe two 'if they were very fond of each other', which was a family joke. Roger's mother looked at Roger and then at her husband.

'Roger says he's willing to sleep in his old room,' she said doubtfully.

'Are you, Rodge? Really? Don't if you'd rather not. I can sleep sitting up. . . .'

'It's okay, Dad. I'm not worried about it, honestly.'

He got a kiss from each of his parents and the torch from his father. Then they all went their separate ways.

Roger stood at the door of his room and waited for panic. None came. He opened the door with only normal caution and shone the torch all around the little room. The only traces of the visitation of the snake was a curious dent in his pillow, narrower than that made by a human head. That gave him a slight shiver, but nothing much.

He entered, walked past the bed and into the farthest and, by day, darkest corner, beyond the bed's foot. He shone the torch upward.

Yes. There it was. A black shadowy hole about the size of a large rat hole or a small rabbit hole. Right in the corner of the ceiling, eight or nine feet off the ground. He turned, pushed the bed across the floor till it stopped against the far wall, and climbed on to it. But it was too low. He couldn't do more than shine his torch straight up through the hole from a distance of about a foot.

He couldn't see anything except the thickness of the ceiling. He could make out the broken laths and the edge of a wooden beam or joist. Then the light got lost in blackness.

Suddenly he thought, *She's up there. If she's still awake she'll see the light. She might be frightened.* . . . He switched the torch off and stood on his bed in the dark, listening.

Not a sound except the rain and wind.

She knows, he thought. *She knows that I know. Perhaps she wanted me to find out. Otherwise why did she keep coming into my room? Perhaps she can't help what she does when she's . . . like that. Or perhaps . . . perhaps she's lonely. Or frightened.*

He crouched down on the bed, thinking.

Roger had always been fascinated by people who were different. Geniuses. Freaks. Handicapped people. People who had to face life with immense problems – even being brilliant was such a problem – which set them apart from others. He would always watch television programmes about such people. His family teased him about it. The twins called him morbid, especially if it was about somebody whose difference was visible or awful. He had no answer. Maybe it was morbid. But it seemed as if he couldn't get enough of trying to imagine himself into their bodies and minds.

How – *how* could you cope with being so different? How did it *feel*, how could anyone bear it?

'We're just ordinary,' these people often said in interviews. 'We want what everybody wants. We just want not to be laughed at, not to be stared at, to be accepted.' Roger always wanted to say to them, *But you can't expect people not to stare, when you're so different – so interesting*. He never had the least inclination to laugh, though. That was something he simply couldn't understand, how people could laugh. It wasn't just that it was cruel or rude. You'd have to have no feelings at all.

One of the worst fights he'd ever had with his sisters had happened about three years ago. He was reading in one of the Sunday supplements about a little boy who had hardly any face, due to a disease. That really was horrific. He was staring at a photo of this kid with a hole in the middle of his face where his nose ought to be, and feeling sick, not with disgust so much as with pity, when Polly came up behind him and looked over his shoulder. She let out a great '*Yeuchh!*' and began to act up, making sick noises and throwing herself about the room. That made Emma come to look, though Roger tried to cover the photos with his hands, and she did the same as Polly.

And Roger had simply seen red. He had leapt up from the table like a madman and grabbed the pair of them and banged their heads together. Of course they'd started yelling the place down, and that maddened him more, and he had just begun bashing them both, only luckily he was too blazing furious to aim his blows and most of them had missed, or he might have really hurt them. Someone had to come and pull him off.

Later his father had a talk to him.

'Do you really hate your sisters?'

'No.'

'You behaved as if you did.'

'Well, I hated them when they acted stupid about that little boy.'

'You attacked them for reacting differently from you. That's being intolerant. That's being a bigot.' Bigot was his father's stongest word for anyone he really disapproved of.

Nobody seemed to understand. 'It's not as if the little boy could hear and be hurt by anything they said,' said his mother. 'But you were ready to hurt them. That makes you worse than they were.' Roger felt crushed and miserable for days afterwards. He had never allowed himself to lose his temper like that again – he'd frightened himself with the violence of his anger.

Now he crouched on his bed and thought about some of this. It was as if all the years when people who were different had fascinated him, when he had struggled to understand them and feel what they felt, at least a bit, had prepared him for Melusine. Of course Melusine had a problem worse than any one he'd ever heard of.

Did her father know?

Of course he did.

The first night – when Roger had seen the movement under the bed in his room and called the others – Monsieur Serpe had gone white in the face, he had vanished back through the connecting door. Perhaps he had gone upstairs to Melusine's room to – to what? Be angry with her? Tell her she mustn't frighten the visitors? Punish her? But what if she couldn't help it? What if it was like Dr Jekyll and Mr Hyde, what if she had no choice, what if it just – happened?

Had it 'just happened' this afternoon, on the canal?

No. She must have made a decision to save Polly. A conscious decision. Or maybe – maybe danger triggered it.

So that other part of her wasn't evil. No more than she was. She was just – like those others, ordinary in her head, but – handicapped. Wanting to be like everyone else, but cursed with this *thing*, that overtook her, that she could do nothing about, that set her apart from the rest of the world.

Poor Melusine! he thought. Poor, poor thing!

And he understood why he had no more fear of her, or even of the creature she sometimes was. The fear had just got lost in pity.

14   *The Fallen Sentry*

He slept very late the next morning. Just for once, the twins were up ahead of him. The first he knew of morning was Emma, bursting into his room.

'Hey, Rodge! Guess what? One of your old gateposts has fallen down!'

Roger opened his eyes and stared at Emma. She stopped dead and stared back.

'You look funny,' she said uneasily. 'Are you ill or something? What's up?'

He didn't answer. He sat up slowly in bed. His eyes went to the corner of the ceiling. It was all true. He'd been dreaming of it all night long and had woken with the idea that the whole business had been a dream. But the hole was there. He lay down again.

'Don't you want to come and see?'

'See what?'

'The gatepost! It's flat on its face! The wind must've blown it over.'

Roger said slowly, 'I thought it would.'

Emma started to go, then lingered. 'Are you okay? Why don't you get up?'

'I don't want to.'

'Oh . . . !'

She trailed out, saying aggrievedly to someone in the kitchen, 'It's Rodge who's being lazy today, but you don't say anything about *that*.'

The door closed. Roger lay still, watching the hole, knowing nothing would happen now but still watching, unable to come to grips with the thing this morning as he had so successfully in the stormy darkness of the night before. Today the sun streamed in through the round window on to his bed; he could hear his family chatting in the kitchen, his mother banging about with frying pans and cutlery; he could smell toast and bacon, and it was impossible, all of this, and – *that*. They couldn't both exist in his small world. He didn't want to get up and cope with the fact that they might.

He tried putting it into words, mouthing them without sound:

I have a friend who can change into a snake.

No. That sounded too much a matter of choice. He tried again.

I have a friend who changes into a snake.

When?

At night?

When she's unhappy?

When there's danger?

When she's angry and can't do anything about it?

When her father –

The door thudded open. Roger's concentration broke jarringly.

'Come on, darling! Breakfast. It's a gorgeous day.'

Roger got up slowly. He felt very strange. His body didn't want to obey him and moved slowly, achingly, like an old man's. He forced it to get dressed; every little movement was an effort. He realized he was reluctant to go out of this room and face the noisy rough-and-tumble of the breakfast table.

But there was no option.

At breakfast he kept very quiet. Polly was up. Her head bandage had come undone in the night, but the bump had gone down and she looked more or less as usual. She certainly behaved as usual, bickering with Emma over who was to have the last of the English cornflakes and then turning her attention on Roger.

101

'Why are you so dopey this morning? Anyone'd think it was you who nearly got drowned!'

This remark struck Roger as another crack about his courage and he felt himself grow hot. But he couldn't muster enough resentment to answer. He had no appetite, and this caused his mother to notice his withdrawn manner.

'What *is* eating you this morning, darling? You're looking a bit miz, I must say, and you're picking.'

'Did anything untoward happen in that mysterious room of yours last night?' asked his father.

'I'm okay,' said Roger. 'Just not hungry.' He got up. 'I think I'll go and look at the gatepost.'

'Wait,' said his father unexpectedly. 'I'll come with you.'

They went out through the French windows. It was another hot, humid morning; the heavy rains of the night were now being sucked up into the atmosphere in the form of mist. But the heat was burning it off. Already the leaves of the trees had stopped dripping and the slate roof of the chateau was bone dry.

His father was looking at it, too. 'Hard to imagine that roof was leaking like a sieve last night,' he remarked. 'Had to tackle 'Dr Fell' this morning I'm afraid. Didn't enjoy that much, I must say.'

Roger turned to him so quickly he ricked his neck. 'Who? You mean Monsieur Serpe?'

'Yup. About the leak, and the power going off.'

'What – what did he say?'

'Oh . . . apologized, at least I think he did, but in a very grumpy sort of way. He's an ill-natured fellow. Said he'd come and try to fix it.'

'Why was the bedroom ceiling leaking?'

'He said the roof's in a bad state. They obviously can't afford to have it properly dealt with. He said the rain comes in all over the chateau in a really bad storm.'

'In the tower, too?'

His father glanced at him.

102

'What's your interest in the tower?'

'Just that Melusine wouldn't show it to me, that's all.'

'Aha.'

They'd come in sight of the gateposts by now, and Roger saw at once that only one was visible from this distance. It looked lonelier than ever, all on its own. Without waiting to reach the drive, he cut away from the track at an angle and ran through the grass with his father following more slowly, till he reached the fallen giant.

It lay cracked into three or four large pieces. But that wasn't what Roger was staring at as his father came up.

'Look, Dad,' he said, pointing.

'Good God,' said his father.

There was a deep pit where the pillar had stood. It went down into the earth. They both peered down into it but couldn't see the bottom.

'It looks like an old well,' said his father. 'See? It's round.'

'But why would anyone build a gatepost on top of a well?'

'Maybe to stop people falling into it. Or maybe they didn't know it was there. It might already have been covered over. Look, the pillar, when it fell, dragged all sorts of masonry up with it.'

His father straightened up and stared at the chateau lying long and low in the sunlight.

'I told you there's a lot of history lying around these parts,' he said thoughtfully.

'What do you mean?'

'Well, you know the French Revolution? A lot of the people around here didn't go along with it. They were still loyal to the monarchy. They just wouldn't accept that the King and the aristocrats were dead or exiled. These loyalists held out here in the Vendée region for years, and the revolutionaries had to root out pockets of resistance, village by village. . . . Very bitter business. No holds barred. . . . There might have had to be hiding places, escape routes. . . .'

'Do you mean this could be an underground hiding place?' said Roger.

'Or,' said his father slowly, 'the entrance to a tunnel, leading to the chateau. Or rather, away from it.'

'Can we go down and see?' Roger said with intense excitement. His father, who was secretly just as excited, stood with his hands in his pockets staring at the chateau.

'Dad?' persisted Roger.

His father turned to him with an air of decision.

'Let's cover the hole up.'

Roger's eager face fell.

'But, Dad!'

'It's just for now. I don't want Serpe to see this, or anybody else, till we've had a chance to investigate it.'

He was setting pieces of stone at angles across the broken-edged hole, and training some brambles to hide it. Seeing the sense of this, Roger helped. Every few seconds they both glanced over their shoulders at the chateau.

'We couldn't know from here if he's watching,' said Roger.

'No,' agreed his father. 'We're in full view. We'll just have to hope for the best.'

'His car's not there,' Roger noticed.

'Hey, that's true. Let's hope he's gone for an electrician!'

'When shall we explore it?'

His father straightened again, dusting off his hands.

'It'll have to be at night,' he said shortly. 'It won't be any darker down there by day, anyhow. I've got another torch in the car. Come on. Better get back before the others come looking for us. Not a word to anybody, okay?'

'Okay!'

They walked back along the track. With difficulty, Roger restrained himself from bounding. He felt wonderful; filled, to the exclusion of everything, with anticipation and excitement. For long minutes, the discovery of the tunnel (or whatever it was), the secret shared with his father, the promise of an expedition of discovery that very night, wiped every other thought and preoccupation from his mind.

It was only when his eyes – on their way skyward to see if any renewed sign of rain threatened their enterprise – encountered Melusine's bedroom window, and he saw her standing there gazing at him, that he remembered.

At first he felt a horrible jolt. It was so violent that he stumbled and his father grabbed his elbow. But then, as he straightened and adjusted his step to his father's long stride, he suddenly thought:

Rubbish! It's all rubbish. I dreamed it. I must've. This is true – this, this morning. Rows at breakfast, the broken pillar, the hole in the ground. Stories from the past about soldiers and battles and people hiding. The chateau roof needing repair because the Serpes have no money. I can believe those. Girls who turn into snakes . . . Stupid! Impossible. Forget it.

He gave himself a shake, like a dog coming out of a river. He didn't even notice when Melusine raised her hand in a tentative, sad little wave.

Even before they had reached the far end of the chateau, the sky had begun to cloud over. This put a literal damper on the family's plans for an outing, threw the twins into a bad mood, and turned their mother's thoughts anxiously to another possible deluge with accompanying darkness and leaks.

She said they must drive into the village at once to buy candles, oil for some lamps she'd found in a cupboard, and possibly some plastic sheeting to cover the bed and the good carpet in the big room, which had also been leaked on.

'It's awful being abroad when disaster strikes!' she said. 'Not knowing how to call in the people one needs to put things right. I bet that grotty Serpe man won't do a thing!'

However, she was wrong about that. Before they could get started for the village, Monsieur Serpe appeared with a man in tow, who proceeded to get to work on the electrical supply, while Monsieur Serpe explained that he himself was going '*sur le toit*'. As soon as he'd gone, their father, who was in an unusually jolly mood, burst into song in a strong phoney-French accent:

> 'Sur les toits *der* Pareeee –
> Zat's where I long to be –
> Oh what I'd geev for ay moment or two
> Up on ze rooftops of Paris wiz you . . .'

'It must be "*sous les toits*,"' their mother interrupted testily. '"*Under* the roofs". Who'd want to be *on* the roofs of Paris with anybody? The French may be romantics but they're not suicidal. Come on, let's leave the men to it and go shopping, we've got nothing to eat either.' (Of course they had plenty to eat, but their mother, at the least hint of a crisis, always started panic-buying as if preparing to withstand a long siege.)

Roger decided not to go, which his mother said was good as it meant more space in the car for cardboard box-loads of shopping.

The mention of cardboard gave Roger an idea. He found a box they'd brought with them, and set about cutting some small circles out of its sides with a pair of his mother's tough, short-bladed scissors.

Then he went into his room and stood in the corner, looking up. He wanted to get up there and stuff the cardboard circles into the hole. Having rid himself of the mad delusion that Melusine could turn herself into a snake, the only worry about the hole was that she could eavesdrop on him through it, or maybe, with some reverse-periscope arrangement involving mirrors, even spy on him. The only question now troubling him was, how to reach the ceiling.

While he was standing there contemplating, his father put his head round the door.

'Listen, Rodge,' he said in a low, conspiratorial voice. 'If you wanted to read up a bit on the background of you-know-what, here's the guidebook. I've marked the place. It'll make – you know, *tonight*, that much more interesting for you.'

'Okay, just leave it on the bed, I'll look at it. Dad, did that man bring a ladder?'

'The electrician? Yes, why?'

'Nothing. Just wondered.'

His father went off and Roger heard the car drive away. He went looking for the electrician, and found him in the girls' room fiddling about in a cupboard containing fuse-boxes. The ladder was propped against the wall.

Having no idea what 'ladder' was in French, Roger just pointed to it, pointed to his watch, indicated two minutes, received the man's rather doubtful nod, and carried his prize away.

The job took more than two minutes. He had to trim the circles to fit more or less exactly and then stuff them, three thicknesses, into the hole. It blocked it pretty well, though of course if she were determined she could easily enough push them out again from above. But surely when she saw what he'd done and realized that he was on to her, she would be ashamed and leave them there. It would be a total give-away to push them out.

Roger climbed down the ladder.

That was when the idea came to him.

He was a bit shocked at himself, but the idea wouldn't go away. He stood there, one foot and one hand still on the ladder, thinking it out.

Well, it wasn't so very wrong. If she had spied on him – and he was sure she had – why shouldn't he get a bit of his own back?

A quick recce round the flat and he found what he needed – an odd little collection. His father's wooden back-scratcher which he always kept by his bed because he said his back itched in the night; a small fancy hand mirror Roger had noticed propped on a beam near Emma's bed; and some Blu-tack.

He took a big wodge of the sticky grey stuff, stuck the mirror longways to the straight end of the back-scratcher – it wasn't very firm and would drop off if it bumped against anything, he'd have to be very careful getting it through the hole – and then climbed back up the ladder.

He had a bit of a job prising out the three cardboard cicles he'd so carefully bunged into the hole, but he managed it with the curved end of the back-scratcher. Then, reversing this, he cautiously poked the mirror up through the hole.

He couldn't see a thing.

He twisted the stick this way and that but, from his angle, he couldn't even see the mirror, let alone what it reflected. He expressed his feelings strongly under his breath, and withdrew the stick somewhat sharply.

Too sharply. The mirror caught on the edge of the hole and fell off with a little clink on to the floor of Melusine's room. The back-scratcher, with the Blu-tack still in place, came down mirror-less.

Roger looked at it, appalled. Now he'd done it! What an idiot! He climbed higher up the ladder and tried to reach his hand up through the hole to rescue the mirror – which would tell Melusine as soon as she walked into her room what he'd tried to do. By ignoring the scraping of the broken laths, he managed to squeeze half his forearm through the hole, but he couldn't bend his wrist enough to reach the errant mirror. It would have to stay there.

At that moment there was a knock on his door, and before Roger could do or say anything the electrician put his head in. He stared at Roger, standing guiltily near the top of the ladder.

'*Qu'est-ce que tu fais là?*' asked the man in simple astonishment.

Roger half climbed, half slid down to the floor.

'*Rien!* – er – *pardon* – ' He closed the ladder and gave it to the man, who took it and went out of the room, looking back suspiciously over his shoulder.

Roger felt quite desperate. He'd have to do something. Find Melusine and try to explain. Explain – how? 'You spied on me so I tried to spy on you?' How could he possibly find the right words? There weren't any that sounded right, even in English! It was just a horrible, hopeless situation, and he'd landed himself in it fair and square.

It had begun to rain again. He stood in the kitchen staring out of the window. He remembered Emma's words: 'I hate this place. I wish we'd gone to Newport again.' He'd thought her mad at the time. Boring old Newport where they spent every summer, what was the fun in that, where was the adventure?

But now he thought, 'Yes, Newport's good. Newport's safe.' A few bad things had happened there – their father's car had once sunk to its hubcaps in quicksand and barely been hauled out before the tide came in, and then there was the time Emma had nearly been swept out to sea in the blow-up dinghy – but they were the sort of bad things it was fun to remember. The bad things that happened here were in a different category altogether.

Roger really couldn't think of anything he could do, short of trying to get into Melusine's room to rescue the mirror.

Well, why not? Could things be worse than now?

Yes. They definitely could if he were caught in Melusine's room, say by the ogre. He couldn't shake off the dread he had of him, the look of furious anger he had given him that day in the kitchen.

But the thought of the mirror winking on the floor near the hole simply made it impossible for him not to do something, however risky, however futile. He went outside into the drizzle and walked round to the side of their wing.

Then he saw that fate was urging him on. Another ladder – Monsieur Serpe's presumably – was leaning against the outside of the building, running up to the roof which was right above Melusine's window. You could get in from it easily.

What if the ogre were somewhere on the roof?

Not in the rain. He'd have come down. It'd be pretty safe if Roger hurried.

He was up the ladder like a monkey in two seconds. He reached out, pulled open the window which opened outwards, thrust his right leg over the sill, and next moment he was in the room.

His view of the corner was blocked by a table. Without giving himself time to think or look round, he headed towards it, and was half-way across the floor when he suddenly and heart-stoppingly became aware that he was not alone.

In the darkest corner, furthest from the window, Melusine was lying on the bed silently crying her eyes out.

Roger had grown up with girls' tears. At certain stages in their lives, Polly and Emma seemed to have cried about everything, from a sad movie to a parental cross word, from a major quarrel to a dead goldfish. Tears became part of Roger's landscape of life, like growing up in a houseboat. They no longer troubled him. He floated above them.

But Melusine's tears were different.

She had whirled round the moment he clambered into her room and lay, half-raised on one elbow, staring at him from a face like a tragic mask. Great silent sobs shook her body. And the sight of her shook something in Roger.

His first, shameful, impulse was to flee, back down the ladder, back into his own life, and safely out of hers. But his second was stronger. It pushed him towards her, it made him sit beside her on the bed. It made him do what he had never thought he could do, which was to take her hand – that strange, capable, disturbing hand, smaller than his own – and hold it tightly.

And, as she gazed at him speechlessly and continued that terrible silent sobbing, as if she were afraid to make a natural crying noise, the impulse pushed him further, and he reached out his other hand to her face and tried to wipe away her tears. It was not so much to comfort her, as because he couldn't bear the sight of them himself.

'*Que est-ce qu'il y a?*' he stammered. 'Please don't cry.'

She threw herself face down on the bed. Her hand, pulled away from his, balled into a fist with which she beat her pillow.

He didn't think he should touch her again. He didn't know what to do. He looked round the room as if for help.

The first thing that struck him was the total contrast to his sisters' rooms at home. These were cluttered with posters, clothes, photographs, toys, flowers, magazines, ornaments, plants, pictures, jewellery, books, little boxes and trinkets of every conceivable sort in profusion on every available surface.

Melusine's room was as simple and austere as a nun's cell.

The floor was bare boards, neatly swept, with one small, shabby rug at the bedside. The walls were whitewashed, with nothing on them except a small crucifix above the bed. Roger's eyes paused on this – he hadn't realized she must be a Catholic. The bed itself was made of iron, like a bed in an old-fashioned school dormitory, with a white bedspread on it. Apart from that there was a table, on which were her school books; a shelf with nothing on it but more books; a hard chair; and a small plain cupboard, presumably for clothes. Nothing else at all.

Except for one thing. On the chair lay an object which caught the light. Roger stood up and went over and picked it up. He stood with it in his hand. Then he turned round.

She was sitting up again, watching him. Her crying had stopped for the moment, though her face was still drenched with tears.

'Did you see this – come up?' he asked, showing her the mirror and indicating the hole in the floor.

She nodded slowly.

'Did you – understand what I was doing?'

'*J'ai compris*,' she whispered.

'I'm sorry,' he said helplessly. 'Really. I – '

'*J'ai compris que tu voulais savoir ce qui se passe entre mon père et moi.*'

He stared at her. What had she said? Something about her father. Silently he re-played her words. *Tu voulais* – you want. *Savoir* – to know. Something . . . something . . . and then: My father. And me.

112

But it wasn't true. That was something he did not want to know. The thought of knowing made him cold. All he wanted was that she should not be angry with him for trying to spy on her. That she shouldn't cry. That things could be as they were, before he had become aware that something was dangerously and frighteningly wrong in her life.

He found he was shaking his head violently.

'I don't want to know anything,' he said. 'Don't tell me. Please. Just – stop crying and – let's go and look at the goats – '

He stopped speaking with a gasp. Her round eyes were fixed on him with that curious lack of expression . . . Suddenly the fears of last night returned to him full force. Because, lying on the bed with her body curved like that and her head raised, she looked – she looked –

He lost his nerve. He made a sudden lunge for the window, but as he reached it and was about to climb out he saw the ladder move. Glancing down, he saw to his horror that Monsieur Serpe was climbing it.

He shot a panic-stricken look at Melusine. In a flash she was off the bed and pushing him towards the door. Just as he backed out he saw the top of Monsieur Serpe's grizzled head appearing over the window sill. Then the door silently closed and he was standing on a bare, dusty landing, his heart knocking, his breath stuck in his throat.

He found his way down to the ogre's kitchen – he had to force himself to go in there, knowing no other way out, but he didn't pause to look at anything, not the gun, not the armchair. He just shot straight across it from the door and out through the back window.

The rain had stopped but the grass was wet. He arrived at the flat soaked to the knees and shivering. *That was close, that was too close!* he kept thinking. *If he'd seen me in there . . .!* He went into his room. Through the hole came the sound of

113

voices, one deep and gruff, one faint and high. The gruff one had the most to say. It sounded like a big angry dog barking.

He wished with all his heart that he had left the three circles of cardboard stuffed into the hole.

He wanted to hear the car, to know his parents and the twins were back. . . . He glanced round desperately. Till they came, he must occupy himself. Take his mind off things. And there, like an answer, was the guidebook, lying on his pillow.

He snatched it up and almost ran into the big living-room, which was as far from his own room as he could get. There he drew a magnificent chair like a throne, padded with tapestry, up to the octagonal table.

His father's marker had fallen out as he carried the book; he would have to search for the place he had wanted him to read. He opened the guidebook at random and riffled through the pages that were much-thumbed by his father, the part about the Vendée. And almost at once he saw Melusine's name.

It was the bit he'd been reading in the car when he'd started to feel sick. Now, though with a shrinking feeling of unwillingness, he read the passage through.

'Melusine, after whom this tower and some less well-known local landmarks are named, is a shadowy mythological figure, unknown outside this region. Her origins are lost in the mists of antiquity, but a clue may be found in some old liturgical texts, and by looking closely at such rare representations of her as the one to be found among the carvings around the eaves of her tower, where on either side of her are snake-head gargoyles.

'These are said by some to be her "familiars", implying that she was a witch of the Middle Ages who could conjure demons in the shape of reptiles and other creatures. But an older tale suggests that she is a direct descendent of the serpent who tempted Eve in the Garden of Eden, and as such the incarnation of evil, while at the same time being the instrument of God. What is common to both tales is that Melusine is the embodiment of both good and evil, being a woman – Eve herself, perhaps – by day and a snake by night.'

Roger laid the guide-book down very gently. He stared at the table. It was one of the most beautiful pieces of furniture he had ever seen, outside a museum or a stately home. To calm the trembling of his hand, he stroked its many-coloured, many-stoned surface. It felt like a sheet of glass. Amazing how they cut the bits, how they fitted them all together without a single gap so that, if you closed your eyes, you couldn't tell where the pieces joined.

And the design was fascinating, now he looked at it closely for the first time. Flowers – leaves – intertwining tendrils – geometric borders; like a dense, formalised jungle. There were animals, too, half-hidden so that you had to search for them.

Roger knew something about stones; he'd had a pebble-polisher once, and a book that came with it. That tiger's eye was a fragment of green agate, these tiny fish were perfectly shaped in bright blue lapis-lazuli. And this sinuous form, twisting round a branch, was made of malachite and cornelian, the diamond pattern exactly echoing that T-shirt Melusine often wore. . . .

Roger snatched his hand off the table. But his eyes stayed glued to it. Once again he had that hypnotized feeling as he followed the stone snake's length and saw that, twisting and insinuating itself, hiding sometimes, sometimes camouflaged among leaves and triangles, sometimes boldly in plain sight, it went right around the table, till its tail was back beside its head. It embraced the whole pattern. It was the *main thing*. Yet he hadn't seen it till now. Though it was sinister, like all snakes, with its flat head, flashing forked tongue, round black eyes and scaly body, it was also beautiful and piteous. Doing what it had to do and being hated for it.

Roger put his head down on the snake's head.

'Hi, Rodge! Been looking for you!'

He jerked his head up, leaving the highly polished surface misted.

115

'Hi, Dad,' he said. He cleared his throat. 'Just been reading the guidebook.'

'Oh yes? Good. We got all the stuff – Mum's bought enough to stock a quartermaster's stores. We won't starve, whatever happens.'

'Dad. Have you looked at this table?'

'Yes. A bit garish for my taste, but amazing workmanship.'

'Do you know what it is?'

'Stone inlay, isn't it? They do it in Florence, in Italy, I've watched them.'

'No. I mean the design.'

His father peered closer. 'What do you mean, what it is? Sort of jungle pattern, isn't it?'

'It's the Garden of Eden.'

'Who said so? Where's Adam and Eve then?'

'I suppose,' said Roger slowly, 'that this is after they were chucked out.'

'Did Melusine tell you it was the Garden of Eden?' asked his father, looking at him curiously.

He shook his head. 'It is, though. I know it is. Look. There's the snake.'

'Oh . . . yes, I see it now! You don't notice it at first. Maybe Eve didn't either!' He laughed.

'Dad. . . .'

'H'm?'

'How can something be the embodiment of evil and at the same time, the instrument of God?'

His father straightened up and stared at him.

'Where did you get that?'

'It's in the guidebook. About the serpent in the Garden. I mean, it couldn't have been both, could it?'

'Well,' said his father, 'I'm not the person to ask, but it's fairly obvious that if it had really happened the way it says in the story, the snake couldn't have got into the Garden without God knowing. And He could have kept it out. So it must have been part of His purpose, somehow.'

116

'To get Adam and Eve kicked out?'

'Or just to test them.'

'Knowing they might . . . you know. Fall for it.'

'Knowing they *would*, surely,' said his father. 'God is supposed to know everything.'

They stood together, staring at the table, their eyes following the twisted path of the snake through the forest.

'Then it was all fixed,' said Roger. 'Everything that's happened since the beginning. God knew. He planned it.'

'Well, but you mustn't apply logic to religion, Roger. It's like applying logic to magic or fantasy. People believe what they need to. If they asked questions like that, it would all fall to the ground very quickly. That's why they say faith is so important. That's believing without questions.'

'Is that why you don't believe?'

'I can't believe because of all the suffering. . . . Yes. Put another way, what you said before is precisely why I don't believe.'

After another silence, his father made a move as if to go out of the room, but Roger grabbed his arm with sudden urgency.

'Dad! Is it – I mean, if a person – if she were suffering, really badly so that she couldn't bear it, and God and – I mean, not God or anybody else did anything to stop it, even though she believes in Him, would that explain . . . I mean, if you really can't bear something, and it keeps on happening, you might – you might change, something could break out in you, you could become – something completely different. Could that happen, d'you think?'

His father looked into his eyes.

'What are you trying to tell me, son?'

Roger looked down.

'I don't know . . . I just thought. . . .'

'There's no doubt that suffering can change people. And nobody can tell me that it always makes them better.'

Roger stood still, staring at the floor. He didn't say

anything more. But what he was thinking was, that if they really went away next week and left Melusine here alone with her father, they would be more cold and cruel and heartless than any poor snake in the world.

17   *Visits and Scruples*

That night when he was in bed, Roger was visited.

He heard her coming. The familiar whispering, rustling sound. He waited for the fear to engulf him, fear as old as the Garden and instinctive as reaching out when you're falling. But it didn't come. It started to; he felt the beginnings of it in the little flush of gooseflesh along his arms. But he only had to say to himself, 'It's all right – it's only Melusine,' for it to die down.

She came to him across the bed and he felt her arrange herself, snake-fashion, coil by coil within the curve of his bent knees. At last he felt the weight of her head and the first foot of her length come to rest very gently – as if unsure of her welcome – across his hip.

He reached out his hand in the darkness. This took courage. After all, he had no way of knowing how much of her snake responses – snake instincts – might be working. She might not be able to help striking at him if he touched her. As his hand moved slowly towards her, he remembered how, even as a girl – as herself – she had lashed out at him that day by the tower, her hand moving with all a snake's speed and self-protecting violence . . . But he felt he must touch her now, let her know that he was with her, not afraid of her, that, as much as an ordinary person could, he understood, and did not shrink from her in this awful form.

Besides, he wanted to touch her. Even like this.

The small flat head lay under his hand.

Warm-cool. Rough-smooth. Pulsing softly with life.

He stroked her very gently. She lay still.

He wanted to speak to her. The words he wanted to say were, 'You're all right. You're safe with me.' But he didn't speak. She probably couldn't understand human speech when she was like this. And anyway, it wouldn't be true. She was safe at this moment, yes. That was why she came down here, he knew that now, to *not* be in her bedroom, to be where her father couldn't get at her. She came through the hole in her floor – probably when there was nobody living below, as well – to hide, to be safe.

But Roger couldn't really protect her. Somehow when it was morning she had to crawl back, up through her little escape-hole, back into her own shape, into her own damaged life. *And there was nothing he could do about it.*

For the first time in his life he tasted a kind of despair. Even her animal self had given him her trust. He wanted to turn in bed, to gather her up, to hold her shieldingly and carry her away somewhere where no harm could ever come to her. But he was helpless.

They lay like that, the big reptile coiled behind the boy's knees, his hand on its neck, until his sense of powerlessness exhausted him and he fell asleep. The big snake lay under his hand until dawn. Then it slipped quietly away.

It was only when he woke the next day that Roger remembered about the tunnel.

He was glad to remember it. It was so much easier to think about than Melusine. He allowed himself to half forget about the visitation of the night, though when it did cross his mind it left a warmth, a sense of secret intimacy. But he preferred to think about the straightforward adventure which was to come.

'Why didn't we explore the tunnel last night?' he asked his father privately before breakfast.

'To tell the truth, I didn't wake up. I was knackered,' said his father. 'Dunno why. The air here is very relaxing.'

'Can we go tonight?'

'Yes,' he said decisively. 'I'll wait till Mum's asleep and then I'll creep out and wake you, and we'll go.'

'What are we going to do today?' asked Emma at breakfast.

'What would you say to an artificial sports lake?'

'YES!' the twins chorused, and Roger heard himself join in.

'Can Melusine come?' he asked before he could stop himself, and then braced his mind for the mickey-taking, but it didn't come. It seemed the twins had decided they liked Melusine.

'Yeah, let's invite her,' said Polly.

'Have you seen her this morning?' Emma asked slyly.

'No. How should I?'

'Well, you know . . . you're her lonesome goatherd. Or you were.'

Roger frowned. It was as if the goats had been just a way of getting to know her, and, now they'd served their purpose, he had lost interest in them. But he felt guilty about this. After all, whatever happened – what*ever* happened – the rest of the time, Melusine had to milk the goats morning and evening, and Roger knew that with his help this chore was easier and quicker. There was plenty he couldn't do for her. This was something he could do.

His mother noticed the frown and interpreted it rightly.

'It's still early,' she said. 'Why not dash round now and see if she's still milking? And you can ask her if she wants to come to the lake with us.'

Roger went out through the big room window and took the short cut. He met Melusine at the corner by the tower.

He stopped when he saw her. She looked just as usual, and he knew that when he got closer to her she would smell of goat and milk. It struck him as incredible, this ordinariness, this – down-to-earthness. Watching her walking carelessly towards him he felt as he might have done a few days ago if he had rounded a corner and met a large snake gliding

121

through the grass, its skin the same gold and green diamond pattern as Melusine's T-shirt.

'Melusine?' he heard himself ask, as if he were not sure it was her.

'*Oui*, Melusine,' she said with her little hint of mockery.

Did she know what she did when she was the snake? Did she know that she had come to curl up trustingly beside him in the night, that he had stroked her little head and that they had fallen asleep together?

He cleared his throat and tried to shake off this sense of two realities.

'Have you finished milking?'

'*Oui, j'ai fini* "meelking",' she said, still mocking. '*Merci pour ton assistance.*'

He flushed. She was being sarcastic now about his failure to turn up.

'Would – could you come with us to the lake? *Le lac,*' he translated when she gave him her blank look.

'*Quel lac?*'

'I don't know its name. You can swim there and go windsurfing.'

'*C'est quoi – ce* "windsor fing"?'

'It's a sport – great fun. You'll see, if you come.'

She rested her weight on one leg and stared out at the fields. He sensed how badly she wanted to come.

'*Je ne peux pas,*' she said at last. Her voice was hard but unsteady, and she avoided his eyes.

'Why can't you?'

'*Mon père ne serait pas d'accord.*'

Why should you care if he doesn't like it? Roger thought, feeling anger rising in him. But now her eyes were on him and he read a warning in them.

There was no point in saying any more. He stared at her for a second, and then turned, so that she wouldn't see his disappointment, and walked away. But it was strangely difficult. It was as if a piece of elastic linked them and was trying to snap him back, pulling harder and harder as the distance between them increased. He took a deep breath and this tension eased. It stopped altogether only when he climbed in through the window of the big room.

He ran his hand lightly over the inlaid table as he passed.

The family spent a pleasant day by the lake.

It was not a very beautiful spot ('Too commercialised,' said their mother) but you could have fun there, and there was company. They met another English family which had a boy somewhat older than Roger, called Simon. Simon knew how to windsurf and spent quite a long time trying to teach Roger, but he just couldn't get the hang of it. He kept falling off his board and clambering on again (much to the entertainment of the twins) and then trying to heave the tall, unwieldly sail out of the water. When at last he did manage to stay upright for more than a few moments, the breeze caught his craft and carried it, and him, far along the lake. This was glorious while it lasted and he felt quite triumphant, until he fell off again and suddenly realized he was nearly a mile from base and hadn't the faintest idea how to make the thing tack back against the wind.

Simon came gliding alongside, looking enviably in control.

'Don't even try it, you'll wear yourself out,' he called. 'The rescue launch will come out for you. Just don't make them turn out too often or they get fed up and order you ashore.'

Roger privately thought this not at all a bad idea. He ached all over and longed for a rest and something to eat. So, when the rescue launch towed him, hanging on to the windsurfer, toward shore and he saw Emma knee-deep in the water yelling for a turn, he gave way graciously.

'I can do it, I know I can!' she called. 'Just let me at it. . . . Wait a sec, how do you get on?'

'Just sort of climb on to it, pull the sail upright, and then lean back and let the wind take you,' said Roger, adding with scant regard for the truth, 'It's easy.'

He crawled up the beach to where his parents and Polly were sitting with the other family having their picnics. He flopped on to Emma's abandoned towel and reached for a baguette sandwich.

'Easy, is it?' asked his father sardonically.

'Well . . . when you know how, it might be.'

He rolled on his back and watched, with unavoidable relish, Emma struggling with the sail and then plunging bottom first, arms and legs flying, into the lake. He would have laughed his head off if he didn't know what it felt like. Polly, however, was subject to no such restraints.

'Oh, please can't I try?' she gasped when she had finished laughing. 'My head's all healed, honestly! I know just what she's doing wrong, please let me have a go!' But of course they wouldn't, and she had to be content with a canoe ride and a fairly long sulk.

After lunch Roger fell asleep in the sun. He hadn't thought about Melusine much all day, but now he dreamt they were together in the tunnel, hearing lots of jeering voices above ground: '*You'll never get out!*' He saw Melusine cross herself, something he'd never seen her do in real life. . . . When he woke he realized the voices were those of the people by the lake, enjoying themselves. But still he felt subdued, in the shadow of the dream, and discovered as they drove home that he wasn't looking forward to the adventure to come quite as whole-heartedly as before.

After supper that night, they decided to play a game.

The twins had been almost unable to believe it when they'd discovered, on first arriving, that the splendours of the chateau did not include a television. They had literally never been without one before – even the cottage in the wilds of Pembrokeshire had a black and white set.

'But what shall we do after tea?' Polly had wailed.

'Read,' said their mother firmly. 'Do holiday work.'

'Or play games,' said their father, who loved playing games.

Roger hadn't minded so much. He was not so stuck on TV as his sisters. Pity about one or two favourites, but he could live without it. Besides, he liked games too.

This happened to be the first night on which they'd had nothing better to do, or not been too sleepy.

'Let's play Monopoly,' suggested Roger.

'No. Let's act out titles.' This from Emma, who fancied herself an actress.

'Well, I'm not going to play stupid Monopoly or act out boring titles,' said Polly. 'I want to play Trivial Pursuit!'

'As it happens we're playing Scruples,' said their father.

He had just been given this game for his birthday by his jokey brother. The children had never played it, and, when its rules were explained to them, couldn't see the point in it.

'This sounds dead boring,' protested Polly, while their mother muttered that of course it wasn't suitable for kids.

Somehow or other they got going on it. You had to read out moral problems printed on your cards, and try to guess which player would give you the answer that you wanted. When Roger discovered that the rules allowed the person to give an *untrue* answer – like saying that, no, they wouldn't force their child to take back a record he'd stolen from a shop, when obviously they would – he lost interest. But he recovered it when he found out that you could *make up* questions if you could do it convincingly.

That was much more fun than reading out a lot of rubbish which mainly only applied to grown-ups. So when his turn came, he had a made-up question all ready.

'Dad. If your teenage daughter asked for £5 and you knew it was to get her ears pierced, would you give her the money?'

'Certainly not!'

Roger grinned and got rid of a card, which had actually

asked some complicated question about dirty dealings on the stock exchange which he couldn't make head or tail of.

Next time round, he asked Emma.

'If your drama teacher told you you could have the lead in the next school play in exchange for snitching on all the smokers in your class, would you?'

'Yes,' she said without hesitating, adding defensively, as Polly gawped at her in disbelief, 'Well! – It's going to kill them if they don't stop, isn't it, so I'd be doing them a favour.'

'Doing yourself one, you mean,' said Polly. 'Shnider! I wouldn't shnide, not if I was offered a part in *EastEnders!*'

'I challenge you,' said their father suddenly to Roger. 'That's not a genuine question.'

'How do you know?'

'"Snitching". That's not on the card.'

'Oh, okay,' said Roger. 'I lost anyway. I thought she'd say "no". Fancy having a supergrass for a sister!' He reached for another card.

Emma went scarlet.

'I hate this game! I'm not going to play any more.'

'Where are you going?' asked her mother as she slapped down her cards and headed for the French windows.

'For a walk.'

Roger, feeling faintly uneasy, watched her let herself out into the dusk. Then he forgot about her and started working out his next question. It took all the time till his next turn. This time he directed it at his mother.

'If you suspected that a child – ' he stumbled a little, but quickly corrected himself: ' – a neighbour's child was being ill-treated by her p-parents, would you tell the police?'

His father laid down his cards and looked at him. Then he looked at his wife and waited.

She gave it some consideration. Roger found he was holding his breath.

'Yes,' she said.

126

'Would you? Really?' their father asked seriously.

'Wouldn't you?'

'I'd say that's definitely an "it depends".'

'On what, for heaven's sake?'

'Well, what does "ill-treated" mean? A clip on the ear? A shouting match?'

'Ill-treated means ill-treated, not punished or yelled at. It means the child's being starved, or battered, or – '

'Abused,' said Roger.

'Ill-treated *means* abused, doesn't it?'

'Does it? I thought abused meant – well, more to do with – '

'Sex,' supplied Polly blandly. 'Mum's answered. My turn. Roger. If you backed your car into another car and nobody saw you, would you leave your name and address for the owner?'

Roger didn't hear the question. He stared at his cards unseeingly. *Sex*. It was out. The word had been said and he'd heard it and couldn't pretend he hadn't. He felt suddenly so agitated that he couldn't sit still. He jumped up from the table, knocking it with his knee and scattering some of the heaps of cards.

'I'm going to look for Emma!' he said loudly. 'She shouldn't be out in the dark by herself!'

His father half rose, his face suddenly tense.

'It's not dark!' he said. But it nearly was. 'Wait, Rodge, I'm coming too!' And he threw down his cards, grabbed up the torch, and ran after Roger into the garden.

18 *Into the Dark*

The probing finger of the torch found Roger in the lane, and soon they were half-running along side by side, the beam jogging ahead.

'What could happen to her?' Roger heard his father mutter, and then: 'Good God, Rodge, what are you putting the wind up me for? She's perfectly okay!'

'I didn't say she wasn't.'

'You hinted – you're always giving me the creeps with your mad, melodramatic ideas!' He forced himself to slow to a walk, but when Roger kept up his speed, his father caught him up again. 'Old Serpe's all right, wouldn't hurt a fly! More's the pity,' he said, trying to joke, but Roger didn't respond, just kept running.

'Where are we going?' panted his father after they'd rounded the tower and were running along parallel to the building.

Roger said shortly as he ran, 'To find the ogre. If we know where *he* is, we won't have to worry about Em.'

'And where is he likely to be?'

'Dunno, but I'm going to try the goats.'

He knew that, after Melusine had milked the goats in the evening, her father came and shut them up and got the milk ready for transport to the goats'-cheese factory very early next day. It wasn't very late, he might still be there.

He was. So was Emma.

They were together in the shelter. All the goats had been herded in there and the rough hurdles which kept them enclosed at night drawn in and tied with the thick string. The torch, playing over the mass of heads and horns, of brown, black and white backs, picked out another back, a human one, and then Emma's little white face peeped out from behind it. She seemed to be hemmed in by the mass of goats, and Monsieur Serpe didn't look as if he were doing much about leading her out of the shelter. He looked more as if he were backing her against the rear wall.

'Emma!' barked her father. 'What are you doing? Come out of there!'

'I can't, Daddy. I'm scared they'll butt me!'

Monsieur Serpe had turned, startled. His bristly, hollow-cheeked face expressed – something, Roger couldn't be sure what. Anger? Alarm? His little ratty teeth showed in a grimace that might have been a smile or a snarl. Then, immediately, he began pushing his way through the tight-packed herd towards them, pulling Emma along by the wrist.

'What's going on?' Roger's father almost shouted, as they came clear of the herd and the ogre lifted Emma over the hurdle. She was almost snatched from him into her father's arms.

He gave her a brief hug – more a clutch to his chest – then set her down.

'Phew!' she said, dusting herself down. 'That was hairy. I was trying to help, but I got sort of carried along by the goats and then wedged in behind them. I didn't dare push through. Monsieur Serpe had to come and rescue me.'

Roger and his father looked at the man.

'He was helping you, is that it?'

Emma glanced up at him quickly because of the tone of his voice.

'I called him and he came to get me.'

'I see.'

The two men stared at each other. The rat's teeth were bared again, this time in a sort of sickly grin. Roger suddenly

129

thought of this awesomely horrible man holding Melusine imprisoned on his knees and wanted to hurl himself on to him and hit him hard in his dirty, ugly face.

He took hold of Emma's elbow and moved her into a brisk walk away from the goat pen, leaving their father to follow.

'Did he touch you or do anything to you?' he asked fiercely as soon as they were out of earshot.

'Who?' she asked in surprise.

'Him. Serpe. Did he?'

'No. Well . . . he sort of brushed up against me, but I think the goats were pushing him.'

Roger said nothing. His heart was hammering with hatred of the man, and there was a bitter, biley taste in his mouth that had come up from his stomach.

'Let go my arm, you're squeezing,' said Emma plaintively, pulling away. Roger had forgotten he was holding her.

They got back to the flat to find Polly and their mother playing pocket Mastermind.

'Where did you all go dashing off to?' asked their mother.

'You spoiled the game, just as it was getting good!' added Polly.

Roger grunted something and went straight into his room. He shut the door but didn't turn on the light. There was a faint light in there already. It was a soft glow which came through the hole in the ceiling and fell on to the flags in a little oval pool.

He went and stood under it.

'Melusine!' he called up softly.

After a moment he heard the faint sound of footsteps on the floor above him. The light was blotted out by her head. He could just see the shine on her black hair, and reflected crescents in her eyes as she hung over him.

'*Oui?*'

'Are you okay?'

'*Oui, bien sûr.*'

'What are you doing?'

'*Mes devoirs.*'

'What homework? English?'

'*Non. Je lis un roman français.*'

'What's a *roman?*'

'A book.'

'What's it called?'

She told him the title but he didn't catch it. He didn't really want to know anyway, he was only making conversation to hold her there, to keep the connection between them. It was good to know she was near, that she was busy on some ordinary activity like reading.

'How can you read without electric light?'

She made a little shrugging face. Silly question, he thought. 'You'll spoil your eyes. Why don't you come down and read in our big room? There's a good light in there.'

'*Quoi?*'

He gestured 'down here' and said, 'Come down.'

She gave a little nervous laugh. 'How I can come, from that little *trou?*'

He didn't know what '*trou*' was. But then he saw her hand, slender and brown, coming through the hole, followed by her thin wrist and part of her arm. She was reaching down towards him.

He watched, fascinated. Would she become her other self now, would the folded hand become a snake's head before his eyes and would the whole of her snake body follow? But no. Her arm stuck at the elbow, and suddenly her hand made an open-and-close gesture, inviting an answer.

Before he knew what he was doing, he had pushed the bed into the corner, got on to it and reached up. He could just put his hand into hers.

Their hands met and held in the darkness.

Roger closed his eyes and realized for the first time that what he felt for Melusine he had never felt before. He thought he just wanted to help her but now he acknowledged that that was only part of it.

131

The moment of contact lasted only a few seconds, but he was not in the world of time. He was up in her hand, and while she held him time was not real.

Then she let go and withdrew her arm through the hole, and the little pool of light fell down again. He heard her say, 'I not can to come down. *Bonsoir, Roger.*'

It was the first time she had said his name. The sound of it with its French softness was like her touch – mysterious, heady, disquieting. It made his legs weak.

He sank down on the bed, and sat looking at the soft fall of the light on to the white coverlet. Then he sent his imagination up through the hole to watch her reading. Not to spy on her. To watch over her.

In the middle of the night Roger woke to a gentle shaking.

'Come on, Rodge, time to go tunnelling!'

He was wide awake at once, his toes curling on the cold flags, his clothes coming at him one by one in his father's eager hands. He gave him jeans, not shorts, and a sweater was groped for in his suitcase and pulled perforce over his head.

'It's too warm!' whispered Roger protestingly.

'It'll be damn cold and damp in that tunnel. Put trainers on, not sandals, they grip better.'

They crept out together through the kitchen windows. His father had the torch from the car, as well as the smaller one which he gave to Roger.

There was a goodish moon so they didn't have to use the torches except occasionally, till they got to the gateposts. It was beautiful out, so much so that Roger thought what a pity it was that normally this magical time was wasted in sleep. The night smelt piercingly of goat and river mud and more faintly of eucalyptus, a foreign, medicinal smell. Then his father, who only smoked when he was strung up, paused and lit a cigarette, a French one it must have been, because it had a cigary smell unlike ordinary ones. Roger breathed it in

132

pleasurably – he liked it. The moonlight and the sounds of night-waking creatures compounded the sense of strangeness and adventure. There was not the slightest sense of fear to spoil the excitement. His father was with him so nothing bad could happen. Roger was free to enjoy it to the full.

He pitched in and helped his father shift the camouflage they'd arranged to hide the mouth of the tunnel, and then both of them shone their torches down. There were no steps or ladder but they could see, above five feet down, an earth ledge which might be the sloping beginning of a floor. Roger's father threw away his cigarette and lowered himself part of the way down and then dropped. He played his torch along the floor and then said: 'It is a tunnel, but it's very low just here. Are you prepared to go in on hands and knees?'

'Okay.'

'Come on then, jump – I'll catch you.'

Roger sat on the rim and pushed himself off. His father caught him under the arms. He crouched down. It was hands and knees for him, but his father would have to crawl commando-fashion. The ground was damp from the rain, and who knew but there might be potholes and submerged parts of the tunnel further on? A little whisper of fear tickled his stomach now, but he stifled it.

'Are you all right?' his father asked.

'Yeah.'

'Shall I go first?'

'No, I'd rather.'

'Sure you're game?'

'Yeah.'

'Go on, then. I'm right behind you.'

Roger began to crawl into the darkness, the torch alight in his right hand showing an endless black hole.

Thus began the ordeal of the tunnel.

That was how he thought of it afterwards. At first he kept reminding himself that people did this for sport, for a hobby.

But after a while he couldn't think so rationally. It was the hardest thing, physically, that he had ever experienced. The tunnel went on and on, the ground under his hands and knees sloping down at first but then becoming flat. The air was rank and cold and somehow unsatisfying in the lungs so that he had to keep stopping for breath. Each time he did, he would reach his hand up to touch the roof, hoping against hope that it would have risen so that he might stand up. It never did.

His only comfort – a very slight one after the first few minutes – was that the tunnel was wide enough to turn round in. They would be able to get back, if they met a blockage, without crawling backwards. Water dripped from the roof on to his head and back; he soon had an ache in both. His hands grew cold and then began to smart from contact with the wet, rough ground. Soon his knees began hurting, too. He suspected from the cold feeling in them that his jeans had rubbed right through.

The worst, though, was a feeling – not of being trapped and confined, but fear of getting that feeling. At any time, he felt, he could suddenly panic. Now and then he got strong hints of it, a sense of 'I must stretch, I must stand up!' when he knew he couldn't. And it just seemed to go on and on, endless darkness, endless crawling. The thing that kept him going was that his father was behind him and that *he* was crawling on his stomach, pulling himself by his elbows, which must be infinitely worse.

In one of his breathing pauses, he heard his father say, 'I reckon we must be nearly there, don't you?' in a none-too-steady voice.

'Nearly where? Under the chateau?'

'Under the tower.'

Roger turned his head. 'The tower! But that's off to the right!'

'Can't you feel that the tunnel leads to the right? We're certainly not heading for the front door!'

'You mean, we'll come up in the tower?'

'That's my guess.'

Roger forgot the aches and the discomfort and began to crawl rapidly forward.

19 The Shrine in the Tower

At long last, Roger's torch beam – now weakening seriously – showed a break in the roof of the tunnel ahead. A few moments later, he was clambering painfully to his feet.

His father had to use him as a sort of post to haul himself up by.

'God! That was fairly ghastly, wasn't it?' he muttered. 'Didn't you think it was going on forever? I'll never be the same man again – I ache all over!'

'I thought it was just me,' Roger muttered back.

'Lucky we don't have claustrophobia. Now then. Your torch is just about out of juice. Time for mine.'

He shone the strong beam of the big car-torch upward.

They could make out a vertical shaft of about eight or nine feet with iron rungs up the side.

'Isn't this amazing?' said his father. 'Do you suppose there's a secret door at the top? Let's hope it opens from this side!'

He was all eagerness again, and practically shoved Roger ahead of him up the ladder, coming up behind him almost treading on his heels, his hands grasping the rungs alongside Roger's. The iron felt ice cold and rough with rust. Roger kept taking deep breaths, whether from airlessness or scaredness he wasn't sure. But to see the tower! That would be something!

His head bumped against a roof or top to the vertical shaft.

'Feel around,' said his father, turning to feel the wall behind him.

Roger, hanging on to the top rung, felt the rounded wall

with his free hand. It was very rough, made of undressed stones just piled together, the surface full of jutting-out edges and hollows and lumps. Then he noticed something.

'The curve of this wall goes the wrong way.'

It was true. The shaft was not cylindrical but quarter-moon shaped.

'It's the outer wall of the tower,' said his father. 'We're not right under the tower, but just outside it. These are the foundations . . . Come on, feel around more! There's got to be a way in.'

Roger's holding-on arm was tired before they found it. It was actually no more than a loose stone which yielded to a push. They pushed it right through and heard it clatter down on the other side. It left a hole about big enough for Roger to get his head into, but the thickness of the wall prevented his putting it right through.

There was pitch darkness the other side. Even the big car torch could only pick out the dim and distant shapes of the stones in the far wall.

'No secret knobs or moving panels, I'm afraid,' muttered his father. 'Nothing but ordinary stones. Presumably they just stopped up the entrance each time it was used by shoving the stones back. Come on, let's try enlarging the hole. I bet they didn't use mortar, or if they did it's probably rotted. Ah! You see!'

Another loose rock clattered down on the far side. Now the hole was big enough for Roger's head and shoulders, but that was not enough. Little by little they eased out other loose stones. Roger found the noise as they fell inside the tower wall unnerving.

'Mightn't the whole wall collapse?'

'I doubt it. This part was made to open. Shine your torch upward. See that? There's a small arch built into the wall just up there! That's to hold the wall up when the entrance is open. . . . Come on, keep pushing – all these stones are meant to come out – see how it's getting easier!'

137

Recklessly they pushed out stone after stone underneath the arch-stones and soon the hole was big enough to allow them both to crawl through. Roger went first. He shone the torch downwards and saw the ground not four feet below. It was heaped with rubble and the loose wall-stones they had dislodged. He was able to scramble down easily, and his father was not far behind him.

'As I thought, this is the sort of cellar of the tower, the foundations. . . . There's got to be a way up. Ah! There!'

He directed Roger's wavering hand. The torch's beam shone squarely on to a narrow flight of steps curving round the rough inner wall of the tower, on the far side. They were like the steps in Welsh country walls, just slabs sticking out without support. At the top was a door.

'It'll be locked – bet you,' muttered Roger. But his father was already half-way up the steps.

'Don't be such a little pessimist!' he whispered down. The whisper echoed, like when the girls had made ghost noises in the church – the words seemed to hiss around the damp walls. 'Come on!'

Roger followed him up, feeling his way against the wall. The stairs were only about ten inches wide, and quite irregular in shape. As Roger climbed, he felt really afraid. What if the mortar had rotted, and one of the sticking-out slabs gave way? But they'd held his father, who was now at the top, examining the door. Roger stifled his fear and climbed up behind him. The drop on his left was now about twelve feet and there was nothing to hang on to. He closed his eyes, but that was worse, so he opened them again and just touched the back of his father's jacket for stability.

His father swore heartily.

'You're right. Blasted thing's locked. Not even a handle this side!'

'The hinges aren't on this side either,' said Roger. 'So it opens away from us. You might try pushing.'

His father, more out of frustration than with any real hope, gave a disappointed buffet to the wooden door with his shoulder.

There was a loud cracking noise. His father stumbled and disappeared. Then there was a crash which rocked the stone ledge Roger was standing on, nearly making him fall off.

He threw himself forward on to his knees and the torch flew from his hand. He heard it land on the ground below, where it immediately went out.

The echoing darkness swallowed him.

'Roger!'

It was his father's voice, with panic in it, and then he felt a hand on his shoulder, groping and then grasping frantically. He was dragged from the brink of the top step where he had been sprawled, across the threshold of the door, out of immediate danger.

They held on to each other, and each could feel the other's heart pounding, hear the other's gasping breath.

'God! I thought you'd fallen — '

'What happened?'

'Nothing much – the door fell in, and me with it – the hinges must have been rotten, or the wood, or both – I got such a shock, when it gave way — '

'And the crash! Someone must have heard — '

His father released him and drew a deep breath in the pitch darkness.

'Oh, I don't think so. It echoes in here, so it sounds much louder. The Serpes' wing is divided from the tower by several thick walls, I'm sure nobody heard. . . . What about the torch, Rodge?'

'I – I dropped it down. I'm sorry.' His voice faltered as he added, 'Shall I try to go down and — ?'

'In the dark, are you crazy? Anyway, it's obviously broken. We'll have to feel our way.'

There was an awful silence. They were both thinking of the

139

steps, of the tunnel – of getting back out in total darkness. Then Roger remembered.

'I've still got my torch! In my pocket. There's a bit of life left in it.'

'Oof — ' His father breathed out in relief. 'Thank God for that. Only we must be sparing with it. Shine it now and let's just see where we are.'

Roger fished out the pocket torch and shone it briefly.

They were in a round, empty room. It had a wooden floor, another doorway – and there was a narrow window, high up.

'Switch off,' said his father.

Roger obeyed. Now they knew the window was there they could see a little light coming in from it; as their eyes grew accustomed to the dark, they could see quite well enough to move about the room without the torch. Roger went to the other door first. It opened on to a spiral stairway.

'Shall we go up?'

'Might as well. We've come this far. Only let me go first this time.'

They were both whispering now, aware that they were above ground, on a level with the ogre's kitchen which was divided from them by nothing but a thick wall.

'There must be another door leading outside, or into the big kitchen,' whispered Roger as they climbed round and round.

'That's what I was thinking. It must have been bricked up.'

'Why?'

'Presumably so no one could get in.'

'What's the big secret?'

'Is there one?'

'It's the one place Melusine wouldn't show me.'

'Maybe she didn't know how to get in.'

'You can get in at first floor level. I saw the door.'

'Here's a door. . . .' said his father. Roger heard the rasp as his hands moved over wooden boards. 'Maybe this is the one you saw from the other side. Was it locked?'

'I didn't try it, but I'm sure it was.'

'This one certainly is, and it's not rotten either – it smells like newish wood.'

They kept climbing, passing a very narrow opening in the wall, the kind Roger called an arrow-slit when he saw them in English castles. Looking out, he could see the moon shining over the fields. They were quite high up.

'We must be at second floor level now – hey, here's another door!'

This time there was a latch. He heard his father clicking it stealthily. Then he felt a draught of warmer air. It carried an odd odour.

'What's that smell?'

'Smells like a Catholic church — '

Yes, that was it. Candles and incense. But how could it be?

'If Serpe is trying to keep people out of here, he should have locked this too,' his father said as he pushed carefully. The hinges emitted a harsh metallic shriek which nearly made Roger jump out of his skin.

'Shhh, Dad!' he hissed. But his father had got over any fears he had felt and was now boldly determined to get his money's worth out of this expedition.

He pushed the squeaking door fully open and stepped into the upper room.

It was dimly lit by the indirect light of the moon. At first, as they stepped in, they couldn't quite credit what they seemed to see. After all the emptiness, it was so strange.

They thought the room was a bedroom. There was something like a very small, narrow bed against the wall farthest from the door, which had curtains or something draped above and behind it like an old fashioned bed-head. Heaped around the bed were strange, fussy shapes that looked like flowers.

'Shine the torch, Rodge.' His father's whisper had nothing in it but intense curiosity.

Roger shone the torch and they moved across the round open space towards the thing that looked like a little bed. Halfway across, they both stopped cold.

It wasn't a bed. It was a coffin.

It stood on trestles. The draperies over and around it veiled it and gave it an air of solemn mystery. The fussy shapes were wreathes, a lot of them. They were made of artificial flowers, and beads. At the head and foot of the coffin were tall brass candlesticks the height of a man. Each had a thick unlit candle in it. On the coffin itself stood a little statuette of the Virgin Mary. The whole tableau had the air of a shrine.

'Dad!' exclaimed Roger out of a bone-dry mouth. 'What – what is it?'

Instead of answering, as he might have done, 'It's a coffin, what does it look like?' his father understood the question and said hollowly, 'I don't know, son. I just wish we'd never seen it.'

'But we must find out! We must know who — '

'It's none of our business, Rodge. Come on, let's get out of here.'

They turned to go, the torch swinging its faded light round to guide them. Then Roger let out a harsh cry.

Monsieur Serpe was standing in the doorway. He had a gun in his hands.

20   The Wild Animal

Roger stood petrified – shocked to numbness by this sudden apparition, by the threat. Yet he was not surprised. This was what he had subconsciously known would be the end of it. Monsieur Serpe would shoot him. Now it would happen.

His father tried to force Roger behind him, but it was as if he were fixed to the floor. He just stood there like a pillar, staring with wide open eyes at this monster of a man.

Serpe moved out of the doorway and stood half crouched next to the window. His movements were heavy and deliberate, but the barrel of the rifle – aimed at Roger's father's chest – wavered with the shaking of his arms. The rat-mouth opened and a stream of what sounded like frenzied abuse poured out. Roger thought: *He's mad. He's a wild beast. He'll kill us both for being here, for seeing – whatever it is we've seen.*

Roger's father stood perfectly still, as if any move of his might make the gun go off. After what seemed like hours of the barking French voice, the man stopped shouting, and the muzzle of the gun steadied. Somewhere during the harangue, the torch, hanging at the length of Roger's limp arm, had gone finally out. But there was still enough light from the window behind the man for him to aim and not miss. Roger shut his eyes.

The gun went off with a deafening roar which banged off the stone walls and seemed to hit the ears twice like blows. At the same instant Roger turned inward towards his father, and felt himself knocked to the ground. A heavy weight fell on top of him which he knew was his father's body. Through the echo of the explosion he heard other sounds, a gasping and choking and then scraping, grunting sounds, as of a struggle.

Roger hardly registered these noises. His ears were still ablaze from the gunshot. And his mind was wading through thick terror. His father lay on top of him. *Dead*. Was he dead?

No. He wasn't dead, he was moving. Roger felt him move.

That basic terror out of the way, the next-worst thing was trying to breathe. The body on top of his was crushing him. He gave a heave, caught air into his lungs, and then felt his father put a hand over the top of his head. He knew, then – the relief was like pain – his father hadn't been hit! He had knocked him down and fallen on him to shield him. Now both their faces were pressed to the floor.

Roger wrested his head free and raised his face a little. He did it to breathe better, not to look. But his eyes were drawn to the writhing silhouette in front of the window and what he saw held him immobile.

The man Serpe was struggling wildly. The gun was not in his hands any more. He was using his hands to fight something that enveloped him, something that was wrapping itself round him. Roger didn't have to see the pale reflection of the moonlight on the sinuous scales to know, in a paralysed instant, what it was – who it was. He began struggling in his turn.

'Melusine — ' he tried to cry out. 'Don't – don't kill him!' His father's weight made the words emerge as all but soundless gasps.

Nevertheless, suddenly there was a lightning movement, a falling-away, and the man was free.

For a second he stood at the window, his arms loose at his sides. Then his head dropped back, and for an instant Roger saw, etched in greys and blacks, the tortured face. The black mouth opened and gave out a howling cry. It had words. Then his whole body arched backwards.

Did something on the floor lift his feet, to tip the balance? Could he otherwise have fallen back over the stone sill? Roger didn't know because he couldn't watch. He banged his face down again on the floor in his instinctive will not to see it happen. But he couldn't block his ears to the despairing cry which ended abruptly at ground level. Nor the sibilant rustle across the boards which perhaps only Roger's ears could have detected.

The police, fetched by Roger's father from the nearest town at two o'clock in the morning, didn't believe him at first.

They didn't believe in the tunnel and the sealed tower and the coffin, let alone the dead man. But if they didn't believe this white-faced Englishman's story, perhaps there was something about the boy who was with him, standing pale and shaking and with a blood-stained handkerchief pressed to his nose, in the curve of his mother's arm, and the two bewildered young girls who had been got out of their beds because they couldn't be left alone, that convinced them that *something* had happened that required to be investigated. So they came back to Chateau Bois-Serpe, and there they found it was all true.

There was no sleep for anyone that night, except Polly, who kept dropping off where she stood or sat. The police examined the body at the base of the tower and then went into it through the door at the top of the main stairway. Serpe, alerted after all by the noise, must have left it unlocked as he came with his rifle to see who had invaded his secret shrine.

More men – to include a police doctor and an officer who could speak reasonable English – were summoned on the car radio. Eventually they came. While Roger and his father were subjected to several hours of interrogation, other policemen were taking away Serpe's body and investigating the tunnel. They also opened the coffin.

* * *

Roger didn't find this out for two days.

The events of that night simply felled him. He slept heavily and fitfully throughout the next day. Every time he opened his eyes he roused himself to call his mother, who was never far away.

'Mum, where is she? Have you found her?'

'Darling, don't worry about Melusine. I'm sure she's all right. Just go to sleep. You've had pills. Don't fight it, sleep, rest, please my sweet, don't keep waking yourself up.'

He knew he'd had pills, it wasn't natural to have this heavy, dopey feeling, to have to fight one's way to the surface to ask the essential questions. He fought against the drug, trying to sit up while his mother pressed him back.

'But where is she, you must look for her, you don't understand, oh, please find her!'

'We'll find her. I promise. Everyone's looking. Now go back to sleep.'

When he woke up properly it was night again.

He sat up and put his feet on the floor. They didn't meet cold flags, but a soft carpet. He looked around. There was a nightlight in the room, something he hadn't needed for years. It showed that he wasn't in his own room but the twins' room, and that his mother was asleep in the bed on the other little raised 'balcony'. Actually she was not properly in bed; she'd lain down fully dressed and just dropped off. He knew that if he made much noise she would wake at once to look after him.

He crept up very quietly. The carpet helped. There were none of his clothes around, only a dressing-gown which he never wore, but he put it on now, and his slippers. He crept out of the room into the kitchen.

He found some candles left from the night of the blackout, and took one in an ashtray, and a box of matches, outside with him. The night was still and moonlit. He went straight along to the window of the ogre's kitchen. It was pulled to,

146

but he was able to open it. Without giving himself time to think, he climbed in.

It was very dark. He lit his candle. Then he went to the long table and examined it for signs of recent use. Nothing. It had been totally cleared, by the police, presumably. In fact the whole grim place was tidier, if not cleaner than he had ever seen it.

His eyes went to the fireplace where the gun had stood. A shudder of remembered fear ran coldly up and down his whole body.

He spoke to himself. *It's over, he's dead. There are weird things in this world but there are no ghosts.* It wasn't hard to convince himself because somehow the atmosphere in the kitchen had changed. Now it felt just hollow, as if all the bad feeling, as well as all the mess and clutter, had been taken out of it.

He stood still, thinking.

He'd answered the policeman's questions truthfully, but without volunteering any unnecessary information. He'd said he'd seen Serpe fall backwards through the window. The unspoken question was, why?

They asked if the man had said anything that they had understood. Roger's father replied that he had caught some of the words he had shouted at them, but they hadn't made a lot of sense. Something about privacy and the word for 'daughter', or what sounded like it, had come out several times. He'd also thought he'd heard *sacre*, holy, and *pur*, pure. A lot of the rest was simply what sounded like swearing.

'And as he fell, Monsieur,' asked the officer, 'he speak something then?'

'Yes,' Roger's father had said. 'I did hear his words then, quite clearly.'

The officer poised his pencil over his small notebook. 'Well, Monsieur?'

'He cried out, "*Donnez-moi mes filles*,"' he answered.

'"*Donnez-moi mes filles?*" You are sure he said those words?'

'Yes, I'm sure.'

'But, you understand, "*mes filles*" is for more than one daughter. It is, how you say? – in the plural.'

'Yes, I know.'

'Also, what does it mean, "Give me my daughters"?'

Nobody had any solutions.

The policeman asked a lot about where Roger and his father had been at the time, but although he had plenty to say on the subject of trespass, something he seemed to take very seriously, he didn't really suspect that either of them had had anything to do with the fatal fall, because it was clear, from the disturbed dust on the floorboards, where Roger and his father had been lying.

The police were puzzled about some other marks but they didn't ask Roger about them.

So he hadn't betrayed Melusine. He wished in a way they had asked him, so that he could have withstood their questioning and shielded her. Because he knew perfectly well that she had saved them. She had stolen up to the tower in her snake form and launched herself at Serpe just as he was about to fire, spoiling his aim (they'd found the bullet mark in the wall a foot from where Roger's father had been standing.) Then she had set upon him.

Why had she never done that before? It would have been the obvious way of protecting herself. But he *was* her father. Perhaps it had taken a life-or-death situation to make her lose her sense of this taboo against hurting him.

Whether she had been partly responsible for his actual death or not, what must she be feeling about it? Did she even know what had happened? If she didn't know, if she had no memory of the events when she changed back into her normal self, why had she disappeared? He knew she had gone, because otherwise his mother would have brought her to see him, to put his mind at rest.

He had come to the kitchen because he felt almost certain that she hadn't really gone far.

After all, where would she go? Where could she go?

She must be in the chateau somewhere.

He searched for her. High and low. Throughout that vast, echoing, eerie place, he walked the corridors and opened doors and shone his candle into nooks and cupboards and old chests. He walked the length of the great ballroom and opened the oak window seats. Every now and then he would call her in a low, imploring tone:

'Melusine! Melusine, come on, it's okay, it's me!'

The moon set and only his candle, sinking into a pool of wax, lit his way.

At last he came to the curved door where Melusine had struck down his arm. The door to the tower. Well, she wouldn't be there, wherever she was. Yet something drew him to look again at that upper room.

He climbed the spiral stairs slowly. The candle was nearly burnt out, but then, it was almost dawn; through the arrow-slit he could see the sky greying in the east and a cool, clean wind ruffled his hair as he passed.

The door to the upper room was ajar. It was empty. The trestles, the coffin, the tall church candlesticks, the veiling were all removed. Even the churchy smell was blowing away.

Only a single small wreath had been overlooked. It lay just where the coffin had been. Roger walked over and crouched on his heels to look at it, the only relic of Monsieur Serpe's mysterious shrine.

A faint perfume came up from the flowers.

Surprised, he touched them. They were not artificial like the others. They were fresh. Nor was this little offering anything like the big, garish funeral wreaths that had surrounded the coffin. It was a simple circlet of wild flowers, woven into a base made of –

Roger stood up suddenly. He knew where she was.

His abrupt movement flooded the candle flame with liquid wax and extinguished it. But he didn't care. Dawn light was coming through the window now. He started out of the room.

As he went, he trod on something, something dry that

crackled under his bedroom slipper. He stooped and touched it. Then he laid down the ashtray with the dead candle in it and felt around on the floor. There was more of the crackly stuff. He lifted a section of it; it trailed from his hand, something long and crisp and empty. He carried it to the window through which the man had fallen.

It was quite perfect in its way. A tube of scales, torn only here and there – a beautiful, transparent thing – a shadow of a snake.

Roger examined it as much as he could in the poor light. He wanted very much to keep it. But he knew he mustn't. Someone might see it, might ask, might put pressure on him. . . . He rolled the shed skin up carefully and carried it with him outdoors.

On his way round the building to the goat-pens, through growing daylight, he looked for a place to hide the snake-skin where it would never be found. He passed the big dung-heap where the stable straw was shovelled. He found a stick and dug a hole and buried the shed skin in the hot interior of the pile, where it would quickly rot away. He felt an immense relief, as if something bewildering and terrible had gone for ever.

21   The Dawn Search

The goats were all lying in the straw of the enclosure half asleep. Only a few of them got up when he came among them. He dared not use the candle here for fear of setting the straw and hay on fire, but in any case it was getting light. He wandered about among the flock, peering into the dark corners by the back wall, though it was fairly obvious she couldn't be here. One of the little goats wandered after him and he turned and stroked her head. The goats had been the first link between him and Melusine. He whispered, 'You know where she is – if you could talk – ' But that was stupid.

He opened the bottom half of the split door into the dairy, and ducked under the top part to enter. Here he could light the candle. He stood for a while with it flickering over the bench where they had sat the day she cried, and the flies had crawled over her bare knees. Later, in her bedroom, he had seen her crying again, and that was the closest he had come to her. He realized with a shock that some part of him had enjoyed her tears.

His eyes went to the nail on which hung the thick swatch of coarse string the ogre had used to tie the hurdles together, and which Roger had used for tethers. It was this that Melusine had twisted and coiled to make the foundation of her tiny wreath, sticking the wild flowers through it till they covered the front of it. He knew it was she who had made it, and he imagined her creeping up to the tower to leave it on the floor, an echo, a memorial.

Whose body had been in the coffin? It must have been

151

someone she loved. . . . Why had they not been properly buried? What was the secret behind that weird shrine? No wonder Melusine had struck his hand the first day, when he had reached toward the door of that grim, forbidden place. What secret had she been carrying, and for how long, apart from her own terrible secret?

Not for the first time, Roger seemed to feel the weight of her pain in his own heart. He was too young to feel so much. He tried to lift it with a deep sigh, but it wouldn't move.

And then something seemed to twang in his breast like a note of warning.

At the back of his mind had been the notion that now that it was all over – the ogre dead – she would be happy, relieved – free. But in that case, why was she hiding?

Suddenly it was as if his thoughts and feelings dropped several notches deeper, into greater understanding. The ogre, however bad, however *mad*, was Melusine's father. Whatever he did to her, whatever terrible mysteries surrounded him and his life with her in this place, there were normal things too. Everyday things. Trips to the coast, meals together, washing up, the shared work with the goats. Companionship. . . .

Roger's father had hinted that the trouble was that the two of them were alone here together. Isolated, thrown back on each other's company. . . . Because of this, the ogre had 'grown too fond' of Melusine. But what about her? Did she hate him, as Roger had been sure she must, simply because Roger himself did, and because what he suspected of their relationship was hateful?

Or might she, in between hating her father, love him in some sadly awful way because she had no one else?

In which case, his sudden death might not be a simple release for her. She would be shocked. She would almost certainly be frightened about what would become of her now. Knowing this, even in his dopey state yesterday, was what

152

had made Roger so anxious about her. But what if she were also grieving?

What if, now the most important person – perhaps the only important person – in her life was suddenly gone, she felt she had nothing left? What if the weight Roger felt in his heart were so heavy in Melusine's that she hadn't felt able to go on living?

What if that pathetic little wreath were not only for the mysterious body in the coffin, but for her father?

What if it were for herself?

As this thought surfaced, he panicked. He began to hunt for her feverishly, irrationally. He dropped the candle and, with both hands now free, he began throwing empty churns on their sides, wrenching aside piles of wooden boxes and sweeping tools and other things off deep shelves with his arms. The noise and confusion were pointless – there were no serious hiding places at all – but somehow he needed to give way to violent action.

When he'd reduced the dairy to chaos he stood in the midst of it, panting and staring round with wild eyes. In one corner he noticed a pitchfork which had escaped his fury. He hurled himself at it to knock it to the floor and then he stopped.

Beside it was an opening in the wall covered with a bit of sacking. He thrust this aside and found himself in a small, low shed full of bales of hay and straw.

The smell of it halted him and soothed his furious destructive mood. It was such a good smell, full of natural sweetness. Daylight was creeping in through a large opening facing the paddock. He could hear the birds beginning to sing outside and the goats stirring. Normality and a new day.

And as his rage left him, like a reward for calm he saw her. Only one bare foot at first. High up amid the bales. He climbed them like big soft stairs and peered down at her in the dusty dimness.

His heart was beating thickly because of his earlier fear that she had harmed herself, but as soon as he could see her

153

fully he knew she was all right, just fast asleep. She had hidden herself carefully under a layer of hay but she must have stuck one foot out while she slept, an unconscious signal to him to find her.

He looked at her for a while, just savouring his relief. Then he reached down over the topmost bale and touched her shoulder.

She woke and sat up in a flash.

There was no sunlight yet in the shed. But as she rose up out of the hay he gasped. She seemed to gleam. Her hair, for the first time in his knowledge of her, was out of its plait and hung loose round her face and over her shoulders. She had been lying in the dusty hay for hours, yet it shone, black and clean and beautiful. It softened her face. The skin of her face and arms glowed as if they'd been polished.

As he stared at her he found himself thinking of Kaa in *The Jungle Book* after the great python has shed his skin. Melusine had emerged from her snake self, she was all human now, and that shedding had taken away the snake look she had had, leaving her almost supernaturally new and beautiful. Her eyes were still round, but now they were not button-like and reptilian any more. They were warm and glowing, even though a little swollen with sleep and weeping. Her mouth was no longer a straight cut in her face but had softened. It was as if, before, she had always been biting her lips, but now he could see them clearly.

He could also see, through her new beauty, that she was stricken with shock and sorrow and the aftermath of terror.

'*Comment ça va?*' he asked her softly. 'I've been looking for you. *J'ai cherché toi*,' he said awkwardly, still gazing at her in a sort of astonishment.

'*Mon père est mort*,' she whispered at once, as if this answered everything he might ask her, and he knew he had guessed at least some of her feelings.

'I know. Come on.'

He stood from his crouch and helped her over the top bale

154

and down the bale-steps to the ground. He noticed at once that her skin was different. It didn't have the snake-feel any more. It was a girl's hand that he held.

He led her back through the sunlight to his family.

No one knew how to treat her when they first saw her. It was clear to Roger that they all noticed the difference in her. His mother could hardly believe her eyes but she said nothing, simply drew Melusine into the kitchen and sat her down, put her own cardigan round her shoulders and found her something to eat and drink. His father's jaw dropped when he saw her, then he pulled himself together and went to tell the police officer who was still on duty in front of the chateau.

The twins simply gazed and gazed, sitting on either side of Melusine at the table. Emma actually reached out and touched her hair. Melusine didn't seem to notice. She was eating and drinking slowly what was put in front of her, keeping her face down. Her hair swung forward on either side and hid her eyes from the twins, but Polly signed with a finger down her cheek to Emma: 'Don't, she's crying.' For once they were tactful, and got up quietly and went away.

But when Roger began to follow, thinking that Melusine probably didn't want anyone there, she stopped eating and looked at him sharply, pleadingly, through tear-filled eyes: *Don't go!* He swallowed and sat down again opposite her.

His mother said, 'Where was she?'

'In the shed where the goats' food and bedding is.'

His mother, in a distant sort of voice, said, 'What'll happen to the goats now, I wonder?' She was very fond of animals. Still, it seemed an odd thing to be worried about. Wasn't she worried about what would happen to Melusine? It was – when all else was said and done – the only thing that seemed to Roger to matter now.

The doctor came back, and with him another man, a well-dressed middle-aged Frenchman. He introduced himself as 'Maître Gérard – the *notaire* of the departed.'

'That means he's Serpe's lawyer,' muttered Roger's father. 'He's come to see us because I told the police that we're looking after Melusine.'

The doctor tried to give Melusine an examination, but she wouldn't let him come near her. She jumped from the table as he approached, knocking her chair over backwards, and fled straight into Roger's bedroom where she slammed the door. The doctor knocked and spoke to her in a kindly tone but she didn't answer and in the end he shrugged, gave Roger's mother some of the same pills Roger had had, and said he would come back tomorrow.

'But we're going home tomorrow,' said Polly the moment the doctor had gone.

The family, who were all gathered in the kitchen, stared bleakly at each other. They were all thinking the same thing – they would be leaving this place with all its frightening associations, returning to their familiar safe lives. But there was Melusine. What about Melusine?

'What about Melusine?'

It was Roger who voiced the question. And they all turned their faces to look at Maître Gérard, who was standing near the stove looking smooth but out of place. Roger noticed now that he was carrying a briefcase.

Roger's father said, 'Perhaps – er – can you tell us what will happen to – to the girl?'

Maître Gérard cleared his throat. 'Is it possible that we may speak – in some place a little more – *convenable?*' He made a wafting-away gesture at the sink, the stove. . . . Evidently he wasn't accustomed to legal consultations in kitchens.

Roger's father led the way through into the big room, and they all – except Roger – sat in the fine chairs around the Garden of Eden table. Roger lingered in the doorway. He desperately wanted to hear what would be said now, but he also didn't want to be out of earshot of Melusine.

Maître Gérard put his briefcase on the polished tabletop and snapped it open. He seemed quite at ease now. He even wore a tight little smile under his thin moustache. Of course, lawyers throve on all this – death, drama, crime – like policemen, they were used to it and it was what they lived by. Roger had to suppress a feeling of dislike for him because he didn't seem to be feeling anything, unless perhaps it was enjoyment.

He began to speak in broken English.

'This most unfortunate happening has make Mam'selle Serpe *orpheline* and also, perhaps not happily for her – the inheritor to all this – ' He made another gesture which took in the beautiful room and all it contained, but also the crumbling remains of the rest of the chateau.

'But she's only a child! What will happen to her right now?'

The lawyer gave a little shrug.

'She will be placed – how you say – in the hands of the authorities.'

'You mean,' Roger's mother leant forward, 'she'll be put in care?'

'No doubt, Madame. What other can be done for her?'

'Has she no relatives?'

The lawyer looked slightly uncomfortable, Roger thought. He began gesticulating more than before.

'The family – you understand – was once a very big one. They own very much land. This chateau – I have seen paintings – in the seventeenth *siècle* it was one of the finest houses in the Vendée. But those days, Madame, Monsieur, they are past. . . . A parent dies, all the land is divide up among the children. They sell, they go away, just one son is left to keep up the building – in the end, is no moneys, nothing, the house, a little ground, a few beautiful things . . . I tell you the truth, Monsieur. Who now inherit this place inherit what you call the white elephant. Many troubles and expenses and nothing to pay the bills.'

'Will it have to be sold?'

Another shrug, this time a larger one.

'Monsieur, I ask you. Who will wish to buy? No. I will take charge on behalf of the young lady. I will sell what I can. I will make for her a trust, for when she is grow up. And the chateau, it will fall to the ground.' His speaking hands made a gesture of finality.

'Couldn't the government – ' began Roger's father. 'After all – it's a historic building – '

The Maître smiled thinly. 'We are here a long way from Paris, Monsieur.'

He rose to go, putting his papers away.

Roger spoke from the doorway.

'What about her sister?'

The man spun round. '*Pardon?*'

'Melusine has a sister. Living away from home.'

The lawyer's eyes swivelled uneasily. He glanced at Roger's father.

'Your son, he has not been told?'

Roger's father looked blank. 'Told what?'

'*You yourself* do not know? The police have tell you nothing?'

'What are you hinting at?' asked Roger's father, with an edge of irritation in his tone.

The lawyer sat down again and looked at his briefcase for a moment. Then he raised his eyes. He looked at Roger's parents.

'I think better your son, he go out.'

'Roger can hear whatever it is,' said Roger's father tersely. 'Please get on with it.'

Roger came closer. His heart was thudding again. The man beckoned him to join them at the table.

'I fear this will be a shock. You see in the tower, the – how you call it – '

Roger's father leant forward. 'The coffin?'

'*Oui, c'est ça.*' He coughed behind his hand. 'I have it from a friend of me, a police officer. It contain the remains of – the older daughter of my *client*.'

There was a horrified silence round the table.

Roger was the first to recover enough to speak.

'Do you mean – Melusine's sister was in the coffin? Dead?'

The lawyer bowed his head.

'But – but how did she die?'

The man said, 'I cannot say with certainty until the inquest. But I hear a rumour that the *pauvre petite* has end her own life.'

'When?' almost barked Roger's father.

'Some years ago, Monsieur. I can guess when it happen. When my *client* tell me his daughter go to live with her uncle in Canada. It was since five year.'

'Why did he tell you such a thing?'

'Madame, is it not too clear? The young girl, she kill herself. The father, perhaps he think he will be blame. He tell every body she has go far away, to live with her uncle. No one ask question.'

They all sat in silence, trying to take this in. Roger's mind was in ferment.

'Why did he keep her like that, instead of burying her?'

'Ah. That I cannot say. Monsieur Serpe, he is – shall I say – *un homme bizarre* – a strange man. I fear worse than that. Such men have strange ideas. You saw how he make for her like a church. Perhaps he go there to pray her to forgive him.'

'Ah!' exclaimed Roger's father sharply.

'Monsieur?'

159

'It wasn't *"Donnez-moi mes filles"*! It was *"Pardonnez-moi, mes filles"*! Even as he was falling, he was asking them to forgive him.'

'But what for?' cried Roger's mother in a strained voice. 'What had he done to them?'

Nobody spoke. The lawyer lifted his shoulders in a last, very faint shrug, without raising his eyes.

'And Melusine?' said Roger's father. 'Did she know? About – about the coffin?'

Maître Gérard got up again and lifted his briefcase off the table. He seemed to be staring down at the design it had been covering. Roger wondered if he had noticed the snake.

'I will not say yes, and I will not say no. But I ask, how could she live here with him and not know? It is better we do not speak of this to the police, *n'est-ce pas?*'

Roger's mother suddenly burst into tears, burying her face in both hands.

'Oh my God,' she sobbed. 'My God. The poor little thing! Both of them! Poor, poor little things!'

Roger turned abruptly and left the room.

He was waiting outside by the lawyer's car. He hadn't yet finished with Maître Gérard.

He arrived in a hurry, swinging his case, and he broke his stride when he saw Roger waiting, but then picked up speed again.

'*Alors, mon brave?*' he said in a hard, brisk tone. '*Qu'est-ce que tu veux? Je suis pressé.*' It was as if he really couldn't be bothered to speak English for just Roger.

'There's an uncle. In Canada. You said so yourself.'

The man paused with his hand on the door handle of his smart black car. His jaw muscles flickered briefly. He looked as if he were angry with himself, as if he'd made a mistake. Roger decided he really didn't like him. He didn't trust him.

'I have no contact with him.'

'But you know about him. You could find out where he is. The police in Canada could find out.'

'For what?'

Wasn't it obvious? 'So that Melusine could go and live with him – if – if he was all right. I mean suitable, and she wanted to.' There was a brief silence and then he burst out, 'If he was okay, at all, it would be better than being in a home! She couldn't bear that, and she'd be all alone!'

Maître Gérard turned to him. His eyes were narrow.

'Did you know before about this – uncle?'

'She told me.'

'You are a friend to her?'

He nodded.

The man was watching him closely.

'She tell you anything more than this?' Roger didn't answer. 'Do you have an idea what has been going on in this chateau?'

Roger stared at him.

'For years there are rumours. Some are not hard to believe.' He looked past Roger at the great grey building with its towers and its slate roof and the lichen on its walls. 'Some were true, as we learn now. But others – other *rumeurs* are the foolish talk of *paysans*. Country people have so little to think about, so they talk nonsense. Do you know this name – this "Melusine"? You know the legend?'

Roger didn't speak or make a sign. He was holding his breath.

'She was a woman that change herself to a snake. And it has been said – '

He stopped. He was still staring at the grey walls. Roger thought he saw him shiver, and then he straightened up.

'If some of these *paysans*, instead of to talk so much, had *do* something – if I, myself – '

He looked at Roger again. 'I will discover,' he said abruptly, 'about the – uncle.'

And he almost thrust Roger aside in his hurry to get into the car and drive away over the rough grass.

23   Roger's Promise

The car drove away. Roger was suddenly feeling very odd. Through a funny kind of mist he saw Emma and Polly running towards him from the direction of the river.

He watched them coming. Polly was wearing a skirt for once, her jeans were probably too filthy to wear; and he noticed she looked quite pretty, with her brown, curling hair blowing round her face. Emma was running behind her. She was a little bit too fat and was puffing, and her face was pink and shiny. He noticed these ordinary things about them as if he were seeing his sisters for the first time.

As they were nearly upon him, he thought flashingly how often he had hated them, each of them separately or both of them at once, and how he had even wished they would disappear from his life. That, he suddenly knew clearly, was like wishing they'd die. And abruptly he found himself sitting on the lumpy grass.

'What's wong, Wodge?' asked Polly, hurling herself down beside him. 'You look all woogly.'

Roger put his head down on his bent knees and didn't answer at once.

'Who was that man?' asked Emma, panting and staring after the black car.

'Serpe's lawyer,' said Roger shortly.

They looked at him. 'What'd he come for?'

Roger raised his head. There were two sharp little lines between his eyebrows.

'I think he came to get his hands on Melusine's money.'

'Wha-at? What are you on about?'

'He said he'd do things "on her behalf". Sell the chateau. Make a trust.'

'What's that?'

'I don't know. Something to do with her money. She's not going to get it till she grows up. If you ask me, he wanted it. He wanted to control it, anyhow. He knew about her uncle. But he wasn't going to do anything to find him . . . He wants to put Melusine in a home.'

The twins were silent, gazing at him. Emma suddenly said, 'Your voice has gone all funny and deep.'

Polly said, 'Why can't she come and live with us?'

Roger ricked his neck turning to look at her. It hurt.

'Are you serious?'

'I dunno . . . sort of. She's okay, if she'd learn English.'

'Where would she sleep? We haven't another bedroom.'

The twins looked at each other. Then Polly said slowly, 'Well. I'd let her have my room. For a bit. Pod and Ed could sleep together, eh, Ed?' Emma, picking at a mosquito bite on her forearm, nodded doubtfully, and Polly said with sudden force, 'It'd be *well* horrid in a *home*.'

Roger couldn't believe what he was hearing. How they had fought to have their own rooms! How Mum had fought to keep one bedroom spare for visitors! And now this. From Poll of all people. And Em agreeing! Before they even knew the half of it.

'After all,' Polly was saying, 'she's lost her dad. Well awful, him being killed like that.'

'Although he was scary.'

'He was crazy,' said Roger. His legs felt better, stiffer. He scrambled up. 'Come on. Let's go and talk to Mum and Dad.'

Their parents had their heads together over the big table, and when they heard the children come in they drew apart.

'Where is she?' asked Roger at once. The door of his bedroom had been open and there was no one in there.

163

'She's gone to her own bed, to sleep,' said his mother. 'I gave her the pills. She'll sleep for hours now. Do her good, poor little scrap.'

'We want to talk to you about her.'

'So do we want to talk about her,' said their father. 'Sit down, all of you.'

It turned out they'd had the same idea. They tried gamely to hide their astonishment that the twins were willing. Their father, like Roger but for other reasons, looked at them oddly as if he'd never seen them before, or not for a very long time. Then he got up from his chair and hugged each of them in turn.

'The problem will be,' he said, 'getting permission to take her out of France. Countries are quite possessive about their own nationals. But with Maître Gérard's help – willing or otherwise – ' he glanced at his wife and Roger knew his father had made the same assumptions as he had about the lawyer's motives – 'plus our own solicitor, I imagine it can be done, though not right away. I've got to get back tomorrow, but I think the best thing would be if Mum, and any of you who want to, stuck around here for a bit to look after Melusine. She'll need friends. I'll go home and set things in motion.'

'It shouldn't be too difficult,' said their mother. 'After all, we're not aiming to adopt her. Just foster her until other arrangements can be made.'

Roger told them about his conversation with Maître Gérard, about the Canadian uncle. Their parents looked relieved.

'Good,' said his father. 'Good boy. You're a clever lad, d'you know that?' And he put his hand on the back of Roger's neck and gave it a shake.

Roger left them excitedly talking about it and went outside.

The ladder was still leaning up against the roof and, unable to help himself, he went up it and looked through the window at Melusine.

She was on her bed, on her back, raised on her elbows. Her eyes were fixed on the window in a kind of horror – she must have seen the ladder shake as he climbed it, and thought . . . what had she thought?

'Hullo,' he said shyly.

Her face relaxed and she slumped back and closed her eyes. She still had that shiny, rinsed look.

He climbed in and sat on the window-ledge, quite far away from her. Now her eyes followed him. They still didn't give much away. He tried to imagine what she must be feeling, and hoped that the pills were drawing a kind of smoke-screen across the pictures in her mind, dulling their sharp edges and the pain they were giving her. He didn't want to talk, particularly. He just wanted to be with her. But he had to tell her, in case she was worryng about the future.

'You're coming to live with us,' he said.

She frowned.

He tried in French. '*Tu – viens – pour – habiter – avec nous. En Angleterre,*' he added. When she didn't reply, he went on, 'And then maybe you'll go to Canada, to live with your uncle. If you want to. *Si tu veux.* And after awhile you'll – you'll feel better. *Tu te senti mieux.* You'll forget the bad things, and you'll be happy.'

She continued to stare at him. Her lips were parted and her breath was coming in little soundless gasps.

'I promise,' he said recklessly. '*Je te promis.* Everything will be okay.'

She moved her head. It might have been a nod of agreement, or it might have been a shake of denial. Anyway, it was a response. He smiled at her. She closed her eyes slowly as if to watch his hopeful smile till the last moment.

Just as he thought she had fallen asleep, she spoke.

'Please. You milk?'

God. Of course. The goats! They couldn't go all night without being milked.

Without giving himself time to think, he said, 'Yeah, okay, don't worry, I'll do it.'

She smiled faintly and slept.

He went down to his father, frowning.

'Dad. I have to milk all the goats. She said.'

He looked up, dismay in his face.

'Lumme,' he said comically. 'How many did you say there were?'

'About three dozen.'

His father stood up, flexing his unaccustomed, dentist's hands.

'Right,' he said. 'Come on, we'd better get started.'

T he twins went back by car with their father the next day.
They didn't want to stay any longer, they were missing
their friends, and besides. . . . But Roger's holiday, if it can
be called that, was extended for several weeks.

Melusine was asked, at the beginning, if she wanted to stay
somewhere else. A hotel, perhaps? If it was too difficult for
her at the chateau? She thought about it for the whole of one
day, and that day they didn't see much of her. Roger caught
sight of her wandering near the goat-pen, once, and another
time in the sunny distance, down by the river and the willows.
He understood she was testing herself, trying to discover what
she could stand, what she wanted. In the evening she came to
Roger's mother and told her that she'd rather stay here, that
she 'had need to stay'.

So that was that. She slept in her own little cell-like room
above Roger's, but she ate with them and they kept her
company. She had things of her own to do. She continued to
take care of the goats. Roger helped her, regularly now. She
showed him how to sterilize the churns, and where to put the
full ones to be collected by the factory (they were very heavy
but there was a sort of porter's trolley) and how to shut the
goats up at night. He became quite an expert milker. He even
began to wonder if he might like to study farming later on.

Then there were the funerals.

Both at once, two coffins side by side in the church where
the smells reminded Roger hideously of the upper room of the
tower. The priest went through some Catholic ritual and if he

said anything about the dead man, or the dead girl, it was nothing Roger could understand. His mother whispered that that was a good thing about the Catholics, they had a trusted formula for everything. Nothing was left to chance. That must be good for the priest when there was nothing nice to say about a dead person.

Melusine sat through the church part, dry-eyed and erect, but afterwards in the graveyard as her sister's coffin was lowered into the family tomb, she suddenly bent double as if she had an unbearable pain inside. Roger's mother helped her and comforted her. That evening they could hear her crying upstairs. When Roger climbed the ladder the window was shut firmly and the white bedspread was hung behind it like a blind eye.

The next morning she came to breakfast as usual.

But she cried the next night, and the next. It distressed Roger very much. Lying underneath he couldn't sleep for the sad sounds that came through the hole. But his mother said, 'It's good. She ought to cry. I'd be worried if she didn't cry. Tears are like an ointment, they help heal wounds. She's very strong. Just leave her.' Later she said, 'Why don't you move into the twins' room?' But somehow that was out of the question.

In the daytime Melusine helped Roger's mother with housework, much more than the twins ever did. But she wasn't very good at it.

She spent a lot of time walking through the deserted rooms of the chateau. Sometimes Roger walked with her. She seemed to be looking for something without really expecting to find it. But she never went into the big old-fashioned kitchen next door. And she avoided the tower.

She and Roger talked, or tried to. About the goats, and what would happen to them. They were to be sold. Roger asked if she minded. She shook her head. He asked if she wanted him to tell her what his house in England was like, where she would live. She shook her head. She seemed to be living in each moment as it came along, doing what came into her head to do, letting her feelings wash over her like waves.

Once she laughed. They were in the dairy working, and there were the usual myriad flies, and she was crouching, washing a churn. Suddenly she glanced up at Roger and put her fingers in her mouth and pulled it long to make his frog-face. She snapped at the flies, copying his joke-act from weeks ago. And he smiled, and she laughed, aloud. But it was only once.

They saw quite a bit of Maître Gérard. He seemed more subdued now, and the tight little smile never appeared. He treated Roger more politely than he had that first day by the car. And one day, at last, he brought news.

'We have locate the uncle of Mam'selle. He live in Quebec. He is marry with a *Canadienne*. They have a little boy who has four years.' He was translating all this after telling it first to Melusine in French.

'And what does he say,' Roger's mother asked, 'about having Melusine to live with them?'

Maître Gérard did his little cough.

'He has express his willingness, Madame. He has write her a letter.'

And he took an airmail envelope out of his briefcase and handed it to Melusine.

She opened it slowly and spread it out on the octagonal table. (When Maître Gérard came, they always sat in here.) It was three thin sheets covered with handwriting. She read it slowly, page by page, while the others sat watching her. At last she looked up. It was Roger she looked at first. He couldn't read her look but it troubled him. Then she spoke to Maître Gérard.

He seemed to let out a held breath in a long sigh.

'*Bon*. That is arrange. It will take a little time, and in that time Mam'selle Serpe can to live with Madame's family in England, *n'est-ce pas*? Perhaps a few weeks only. Then she will depart for Quebec and her new life.'

Roger heard his mother let out her breath in her turn. He knew why, or he thought he did. A few weeks wasn't long. The twins would be able to stick sharing a room for that long, without wishing they'd never offered.

The next day they set off for home.

Roger's father had taken their car, so his mother went in to Niort with Maître Gérard and hired one. Roger was dead against this, knowing how his mother drove, but he had nothing to say about it. They were driving to Paris and taking a plane from there.

Melusine's luggage consisted of one small, battered suitcase. She wouldn't put it in the boot, but laid it across her knees. Roger sat beside her on the back seat and as his mother put the nice little Renault into gear and jerked forward across the grass towards the road, he offered up a brief and heartfelt prayer that this whole adventure wouldn't end disastrously in a French ditch.

As they bucketed past the goat-pen, Melusine looked straight ahead, but Roger's head turned as far as it would go. A neighbouring farmer who had bought the herd was coming later to collect them. For the moment they were still there; Melusine and Roger had milked them early this morning and said goodbye to them, at least Roger had. Melusine had not done anything special. No doubt she didn't feel about the goats as he did. To her, they meant work, and milk – a living.

He looked down at her hands, resting on her suitcase. Soon the tough callouses would go, and the ingrained dirt round the nails. She was no longer an outdoor Cinderella. She was no longer anything she had been till now, except – the inner girl, the Melusine who, from the first, he had wanted as his friend.

He thought, *When she can speak proper English, we can talk. If she goes to Canada before that, we can write. I can ask her things and she'll answer and then I shall really understand.*

It was a lovely day. The sunflowers were hanging their

heavy, seedy faces now and their petals were browning. The sweetcorn had been harvested. The Renault swept smoothly along the good roads, and Roger saw his mother's tense shoulders and hands relax. Maybe she wasn't such a bad driver, when his father wasn't around to make her nervous.

Suddenly she sat up straight.

'Look, Roger! Your mark!'

'My what?'

'Your question mark! Remember? You said you saw it on the way – there's one coming up now!'

Roger sat forward.

Yes! There it was, painted huge and black on the end-wall of a small country farmhouse, seeming to get larger still as it rushed towards them.

'Stop, Mum! I want to look at it!'

There was traffic close behind. But his mother turned the wheel sharply and the car swerved off the road. Roger heard her gasp, caught a glimpse of her white face in the driver's mirror. But it was still a full second before he realized the car had gone out of control. He just had time to think a broken-off thought: *But it never happens if you think* –

And then the car crashed into the huge round spot which finished the question mark.

Roger woke up to find himself lying on the ground with a lot of people round him.

He tried to sit up, but a fat woman with a kind, round face pushed him down. There was something soft under his head and something heavy covering him. He felt weak and fuzzy. His head hurt badly and he seemed to be gasping for breath.

The kind-faced woman soothed him with a rough hand and made comforting French noises. Then another face appeared hanging over his, and a man said in English, 'It's all right, my boy, nothing very terrible has happened. Your mother will be quite all right.'

He struggled in his head. All he could remember was the question mark rushing towards him. He didn't remember the actual crash at all, then or later. He felt a dark shadow on his mind. The man had said 'Your mother. . . .' But there were others, surely? Not only him and her, to worry about?

'What about my dad? The twins – '

The man shook his head. 'There was no one else in the car, only you and your mother.'

Roger accepted this with relief. He closed his eyes and concentrated on the dull, painful throbbing of his head.

An ambulance came and took him and his mother to a hospital in a town called Poitiers, about fifty miles from where they'd started from, but further on towards Paris from the scene of the crash.

Roger's mother lay on a stretcher-bed on the other side of the back of the ambulance. She was awake, but the ambulance man motioned Roger not to try to talk to her. She turned her head on its side and gazed at him. She'd been crying. He stretched out his hand to her and they held hands across the space. He remembered at that point that she'd been driving. Had he been sitting in front with her? He didn't think so. He couldn't picture himself in the car somehow, but it seemed to him his mother's head had been in front of him.

At the hospital they were both carried out of the ambulance on stretchers. Roger was feeling a bit better and felt silly about this, but he couldn't do anything. They were put into little curtained cubicles next to each other, and a nurse came and took their names. A policeman was there too, and talked to Roger's mother. Then a young French doctor came and said they should both have X-rays, so they were wheeled into a big lift and taken upstairs for that.

It was while Roger was lying on the table preparing to have his head X-rayed, having been told very sternly not to move at all, that he remembered Melusine.

He jerked into a half sitting position and the nurse shrieked at him but he hardly heard her. They had to hold him down, four of them, to complete the X-ray business. The moment they let him go he was off the slab-thing and on his feet.

The pain in his head burst out again and nearly knocked him over.

He didn't know what to do, where to turn. *She had been with them.* Where was she? What had they done with her? He tried to run towards the lift but they grabbed him and ordered him to be still and to lie down again. They made him obey them. He began shouting: 'Mum! Mum!' He heard her faint answer from the corridor.

The nurses hastily wheeled him out of the X-ray room and there she was, half sitting on her trolley, staring at him with huge, anxious eyes out of a chalk-white face.

'What's wrong, darling! What is it!'

'Mum! Where's Melusine!'

He saw her face go blank, and for one appalling split

second, he thought, *I dreamt her. None of it happened*. But then, quite slowly, realization came into her eyes.

'I'd forgotten her. Oh, how could I? I don't know where she is. Don't get upset, darling! I'll ask, I'll find out.'

'*Couchez-vous, Madame, s'il vous plaît!*'

His mother lay down again. She looked terrible. Roger didn't want to add to her problems. But he must know. He must know!

No one knew.

The doctors and nurses at the hospital were no help. Nor were the police. Roger's mother asked for the ambulance men, but they'd gone off again. Later they were found but *they* knew nothing. The people at the scene of the crash were the ones to ask, Roger was sure. So when he and his mother were discharged from the hospital (their seat-belts had saved their lives, they were told) they got a taxi and, at huge expense, went straight back to the house with the question mark on it.

The man who'd spoken English to Roger had been another motorist who'd stopped. There was no way of finding him again – he'd just gone on. The kind-faced French woman was the owner of the house. She lived there with her husband and children, and ran it as a wayside café.

She greeted them with welcoming smiles, hand-clasps of delight and relief, and no English.

Both Roger and his mother tried, with increasing desperation, to explain to her that there had been a young girl with them in the car (which had by now been taken away by the police). They went outside and looked at the place where it had struck the wall. The big round spot, which was the dot under the question mark, was all cracked and scarred. The woman's husband was running his hand over his damaged wall and looking glum.

Roger said, 'We must find someone who can ask them. If

174

they heard the noise and ran out right away, they must have seen her. They must have!'

His mother was absolutely befuddled. She couldn't make sense of it. She was still suffering from shock and from a sense of guilt for the accident, though she insisted the brakes had failed. It was clear to Roger that the accident, the damaged car, their own narrow escape and his father's probable reactions were at the forefront of her mind.

When he kept on about Melusine, his mother said, 'At least we know she wasn't hurt or killed.'

'How? How do we know she wasn't hurt?'

'Well, obviously – she wasn't there with us.'

'She could have been hurt and still wandered away – '

He stared round desolately. The house stood by itself on a field of sunflowers which stood nearly twice Roger's height and stretched away almost to the horizon. How could he begin to look for her? She could have staggered away from the wreck, into the field, and fainted, and be lying there, perhaps bleeding to death. . . . He remembered a terrible book he'd read once, where a woman was injured in a car-crash and crawled around for hours in the dark before anyone found her. He felt physically sick.

'Mum, we must tell the police to look for her!'

'Of course I've told them, darling. I told them at the hospital before we came back here. They said they'd look for her.'

'But they're not! Why aren't they here, searching the fields?'

But she couldn't answer.

They had to leave the spot – had to get back to Poitiers, get their things, settle matters with the police and about the car, phone the family, get on a train to Paris – get home. These things had to happen, they had to happen now, the taxi was still there, waiting to carry them back into their lives. . . .

He tried one last time. He went back into the café,

175

cudgelling his brain to produce enough French to ask his question.

'*Madame – Monsieur – l'accident – combien de temps passé – avant – vous – êtes – sorti de la maison?*' How much time had she had, to get out of the car with her little suitcase (she, like him, had been buckled in with a back-seat seat-belt), to get into the first few rows of sunflowers, to be out of sight? (The word 'hide' came to him, but he dismissed it. Why should she try to hide?)

The couple conferred. Then the man said – as far as Roger could make out – that they had been outdoors on the other side of the house and had not come to the scene until they had heard shouts and someone had come to call them.

'*Cinq minutes? Dix minutes?*' Roger persisted.

They shrugged. '*Peut-être –* ' They didn't know. But it was long enough. Evidently, for she had gone.

Just as they were climbing back in the taxi, his mother suddenly pointed to the question mark.

'*Qu'est-ce que c'est, ça?*' she asked the taxi man.

He answered her lengthily, waving his arms as he drove. Roger couldn't take in what he said. In the end, she turned to him.

'It was for a big advertising campaign,' she said. 'A few years ago. Some cigarette company paid people who lived next to the road, to let them paint those question marks on their houses. Then everyone asked what it was for and talked about it and eventually they put posters up saying "The answer's a Gauloise" – or whatever.'

'Oh,' said Roger. He leant back and closed his eyes. He couldn't have cared less. He was feeling again that elastic-like stretching and pulling as they drove further and further away, and from that he knew she was there, behind him. He felt he was deserting her. But he had no choice and he knew it.

He had a voice like a man, but that was all. He was still thought of as a child and must do as he was told.

When they got home to England it was the beginning of September, two days before the start of school.

Roger was seen by the family doctor who pronounced him fit and well. The twins appeared already to have put the holiday more or less behind them; their school (they were in their last year of middle school) had already begun and, apart from having a riveting story to tell their friends, something that infuriated Roger, they were behaving as if nothing out of the ordinary had happened.

When they'd heard of Melusine's disappearance, their reaction had been, 'Weird! Wonder where she went? Oh well, at least we don't have to share a room.'

Roger's dad, after writing to notify Maître Gérard, was concentrating on making his mother feel better about the crash, which was likely to cause quite a bit of trouble yet – the damaged Renault had been examined by the insurers and the brakes had been found to be in order, which was bad news for Roger's mother who was trying to convince herself that the crash was not her fault.

And Roger had to get his uniform, his books, and himself together for the new school year.

In short, he was expected just to forget about everything that had happened in France, and get on with his life. Or, as his father put it, 'try to deal with it sensibly, put it in proportion. You must learn,' he said several times, 'to distinguish between problems you can do something about, and those you are powerless to solve. Those are the ones you must just not fret about. You'll wear yourself out for nothing.'

'But Dad! Where is she?'

'Rodge, I don't know. I wish I did. I'm worried about her too, but *there's sweet Fanny Adams I can do about it*. So I'm going to concentrate on problems I can do something about. Like Mum being all upset. And the accident. And my dental practice. D'you see?'

Roger saw, but it didn't help him. The only thing to do was to keep going, go though the motions of daily living, but inside he was aching and seething: aching with worry and missing her, and seething with frustration and bewilderment.

After a couple of abortive efforts to talk to the twins, he bottled it all up inside him. Got up in the morning, went to school, sat there all day; ate his meals, though without appetite; tried to work and couldn't. He couldn't concentrate. He hardly talked except about absolute essentials because his mind was never on the conversation or on the lesson. It was ranging round western France searching for a solution to Melusine's disappearance.

After about a week, a letter came back from Maître Gérard saying that the police were still looking for Melusine but they had begun to think she must have been abducted. Roger's father didn't read him that part of the letter, but Roger, who was not normally sly, guessed that something had been kept from him, and later found the letter in his father's desk and read the missing portion.

After that he thought of nothing but returning to France somehow. He knew it was impossible but that was all he could think about.

He didn't tell anyone at school about what had happened. But he did need desperately to talk about it, and after about three weeks, when he was still being 'moody', his father asked him if he'd like to see the school counsellor.

'Is she a shrink, Dad?'

'Yes, sort of. Well. She's a child psychologist. "Shrink" reallys means a psychiatrist.'

'What's the difference?'

'A psychiatrist is who you go to if you're mentally ill. A psychologist tries to help if you've got emotional problems.'

'And you think I have.'

'There's something wrong, isn't there? And we don't seem able to help you. Maybe she could.'

So an appointment was made, and Roger went to see her – very reluctantly.

But as soon as he met her, he liked her. She seemed like a really nice woman. The first session was very relaxing. She just asked him to talk about what was bothering him, and because he felt instinctively that she was trustworthy, he did. And gradually, over two more sessions, a good deal of it came out.

He hadn't meant to tell her a thing about the snake business, of course. The further away in time that that receded, the less sure of it he felt himself. Ordinary, everyday life has a way of making extraordinary, unnatural happenings seem incredible, even to those they happen to.

But he told her his suspicions about what the ogre had been doing to Melusine, and she didn't turn a hair about that. She said she thought it was entirely possible. She didn't underrate the damage that such a thing might have done to Melusine, though she didn't dwell on it. She said that in all probability, the reason why Melusine's older sister had killed herself was because her father was abusing her in the same way; and that that would explain why he was so obsessed with guilt that it drove him mad. Roger asked why he did the same thing to Melusine, if he felt so guilty about his first daughter. The psychologist told him that people didn't do these sorts of things because they decided to, rationally and logically, but because in many cases they just couldn't help it. She said probably Melusine realized this and that was why she put up with it.

'But she didn't just put up with it!' burst out Roger.

'Yes, she did, didn't she? She didn't run away, or tell the police or anything?'

'She did something else, though. She changed. She escaped.'

The woman frowned. 'How? What do you mean?'

Roger looked her in the eyes. Could he really, truly trust her? His father had said, 'Whatever's bothering you, you can tell her. She's heard it all before, nothing shocks people like that.' She gazed back at him, her face open, gentle, accepting. He decided to tell her because he couldn't hold it back.

'Melusine could change herself into a snake,' he said.

The second he'd said it, he knew he'd made a terrible error of judgement. Her face altered. Just how he couldn't have said, but the muscles shifted somehow under the skin and her eyes moved, or widened, or something. It was like a sharpening. The gentleness was sharpened.

'What was that, Roger? Say that again.'

He had two choices, to take back what he'd said, make a joke out of it, or press on and try to substantiate his statement. Because he was basically honest and had held it all in for too long, because he was exhausted inside from everything that had happened, he found himself opening up without reserve.

He told her everything. The sounds in the night, the glimpses, the rescue on the boat, the night she came down and lay on the bed with him. The ogre's last struggle in the tower, the marks on the floor, the hollow dry skin he had found and buried in the dung-heap. The psychologist's eyes never blinked while he was talking. She stared at him fixedly, and prompted him with very low-key questions, just to keep him talking. Several times he heard an inner voice ordering him to stop. *Stop.* But he couldn't.

When he finished there was a long silence and he realized she hadn't moved anything except her mouth for a long time. Now she shifted in her swivel chair and moved her head as if her neck were stiff.

'Thank you, Roger,' she said quietly. 'Time is up, I'll see you next week.'

As he left the room he glanced back. She was swiftly making notes.

Now he waited.

He couldn't sleep. He knew he had betrayed himself and betrayed Melusine. What he didn't know and couldn't even guess was what the results would be. Presumably the psychologist thought he was either crazy, or a pathological liar. She would tell his parents and then – something would happen. Not knowing what it would be was the worst.

Every day was a torment of expectation. One part of him thought he might be shut away in a mental home. A more realistic part simply dreaded the look of shock and unbelief on the faces of his parents. Then there was the guilt about having broken the secret – Melusine's secret. And tangled with these new fears was the old fear, which he had never fully faced, but which, in his orgy of honesty, had come to the surface of his mind – that Melusine was dead.

Another week passed without anything new happening. Then it was time for his appointment with the counsellor.

He kept it because there was nothing else to do.

She had changed towards him. It was subtle, but he sensed it at once. This time she didn't just let him talk, she guided the session; she asked direct questions. Not about Melusine or about the snake. They were never even touched on. She asked about his relations with his mother, with his sisters, with his father. Some of the questions were weird, embarrassing, they made him hot with shame and confusion.

She said she wanted to give him some tests, and had made an appointment for him with another doctor.

His every instinct shouted a warning. He sat up straight in his chair.

'Is it a psychiatrist?' he asked.

She smiled. It wasn't the same smile as before. It was a smile that concealed things.

'Never mind these fine distinctions, Roger. He's a good man and he knows his job. Trust me.'

I bloody won't, thought Roger, but when he got home and thought about it, he didn't see how he could get out of going. He was in a kind of trap.

He sank deeper and deeper into depression. He could no longer function normally. Next day he said he couldn't go to school because he was ill. He looked so wild and thin and unlike himself that his mother had absolutely no difficulty in believing him. She had stopped worrying about the car or anything else, and was worried only about Roger.

She sat beside him on the bed.

'Darling, tell me what's the matter. Please tell me. I'll try to understand. Is it Melusine? Can this terrible state you've got yourself in, be because you're – ' She stopped, and he thought the last word for her: *mad*.

But he was wrong.

'Roger, listen. When I was your age I met a man older than myself, quite a bit older. I fell in love with him. Really in love. I know people say it's just puppy love at that age, but I was in love properly. It lasted for years. It was the most powerful feeling I can ever remember. At that age one has no defences. It just overwhelmed me.' She put her hand out to him, as she had in the ambulance. 'Do you love Melusine like that, Roger? If you say yes, I shall believe you.'

Roger shook his head. 'It's not that. It's not like that. I just want to know where she is, what's happened to her.' He struggled to explain. 'I feel like you felt when we hit the wall. No way to go forward. Nothing working to take you forward. I've stopped and I can't go on till I know.'

His mother gazed at him for a long time.

'Right,' she said. 'If that's how it is. We must go back. I'll help you to look for her.'

182

27 The Chatelaine

Arrangements were made for the twins, and Roger and his parents flew to Bordeaux, and from there in a smaller plane to La Rochelle.

His father had to go, anyway. The husband of the kindly-looking woman at the question mark farmhouse was suing Roger's mother for damage to their wall and Roger's father was going to see him and try to get him to drop the action in return for some money. He was thus not in the best of moods, though he was trying not to show it because, as he kept saying grimly, 'Into each blasted life, some blasted rain must fall.'

Roger and his mother were going to look for Melusine.

Of course Roger's father couldn't be expected to accept this plan without some argument.

'If the police couldn't find her, how do you think you can?'

'Maybe the police didn't look very hard. Or maybe they looked in the wrong places.'

'Where are you going to look that they haven't looked?'

'I don't know yet. I'll know when I get there.'

'When you get *where?*'

Roger said no more. But his mother gave his father a signal and his father stopped arguing.

Roger had had a feeling about his mother, ever since the night she had sat on his bed. She was now his friend and his ally. She believed in him. Once she said, 'I think you've got some kind of special instinct about Melusine.' He gained confidence from this, because he agreed. He had a feeling that if Melusine were alive, the elastic-pull might help him to find her.

And she was alive. He was more sure of that all the time they were travelling towards France on the plane, and then by car towards the question mark house. She was alive or he wouldn't feel her pulling. It was faint at first (he didn't feel it in the same way in England) and still fairly faint in Bordeaux. A bit stronger in La Rochelle, but maybe because he associated that town with her. But as they drove (in another hired car) the long way to the Poitiers road, he felt it more and more strongly.

Like an iron filing getting nearer to a magnet, he thought.

He felt better, much better. His mother noticed that his colour had come back. His listlessness had gone. He strained forward in the car until his father, who was, as always, getting irritable from the long drive, told him to relax, he was making him nervous.

They stopped for something to eat at Niort. Roger, who had almost forgotten what it felt like to have an appetite, found he was starving. The French food tasted familiar and delicious, eaten outdoors as if it were still high summer, and the French scene – they ate near the market, and the sounds, sights and smells were all of France – felt almost like home to him. Both his parents were watching him, half anxious, half happy.

'You're reflating like a shrivelled balloon,' his father remarked.

Roger hurried them over their meal and they set off again.

Abruptly, as they drove fast along the open road, Roger felt the pull slacken. He frowned, turning his head this way and that as if listening for a sound which he had been hearing clearly but now was fading. He reached forward and put his hand on his father's shoulder.

'Dad?'

'What?'

'Can you stop a minute?'

'What for? I can't stop here — '

'Please, Dad!'

184

With a sigh, his father signalled and drew in on the shoulder of the road. He turned round. 'Well? What?'

Roger was frowning. 'I want – I want to go back.'

'Back? Where?'

'I don't know. We're going away from — Turn back, Dad. Please.'

'Roger,' began his father in an exasperated voice, 'I — '

'Brian! Please. Do as Roger asks.'

In martyred silence, Roger's father backed the car and waited with ill-concealed impatience for a chance to cross the busy main road and go back the way they had come.

They went nearly all the way back to Niort – about twenty miles – with his father simmering like a volcano, his mother nodding off to sleep, and himself – tensely silent, listening. It wasn't quite listening. It was feeling the pull, testing it, going with it. They came to a right-hand turning with a vaguely familiar place-name on a small signpost.

'Dad! Here. Turn here.'

His father threw on the brakes and made the turn, muttering under his breath, and they drove on for a few more miles and saw another signpost. The car drew up next to it.

'Roger,' said his father, in his I'm-struggling-to-be-patient-but-it's-all-uphill voice, 'do you realize where we are?'

'Yes,' said Roger in a queer, quiet voice.

'Where are we?' asked his mother, waking up.

'Look,' said his father, pointing to the signpost.

'But that's the name of "our" village!'

Which it was. The village nearest to the chateau, where they had gone for their baguettes, wine, cheese and fruit every day of the holiday.

'Roger, are you leading me back to that accursed chateau? Because if you imagine — '

Roger sat perfectly still for a moment, making sure. Then he turned in his seat to face his father.

'Listen, Dad. Why not? Where else would she *go?* She could have slipped away as soon as the crash happened. Just taken

185

her case and run into the sunflower field and hidden. I *thought* she'd hidden, at the time! Then she could have set off and – and walked home.'

'*Walked home!* Are you crazy? It's over seventy miles! Probably much more if she was avoiding the main roads.'

Roger sat quiet, frowning, figuring it out.

'Yes,' he said slowly. 'Why not? We did a twelve-mile walk at school every year. It was nothing! And she's healthy and strong. She could do it in a week, or a bit longer if she was hiding. She could sleep rough, she wouldn't mind that.'

'But the minute she got there, the police would — '

'Dad, the police wouldn't still be there! They wouldn't be looking for her at the chateau! They'd think like you, that she couldn't walk all that way, but I know she could. Nobody would think of looking for her there.'

'This is fantastic. Absurd. Why would she run back there the first chance she got?'

'Maybe she didn't realize till she actually came away from it, that she belonged there. I thought, at the time, I mean before, that she didn't really want to leave. That she didn't really want to live with us, or to go to Canada.'

'What made you think that? It was a perfect solution for her. And she never said a word against it – she agreed — '

'Dad, you don't understand her! Yes, she knew it was a sensible idea, she *wanted* to want to do it, but she didn't. She didn't want to leave the chateau. She didn't tell me that, because she knew she had to – she thought she had to. But she didn't *want* to.'

'Why the hell not? She and her father lived there in absolute squalor! And her memories . . . I should have thought she couldn't wait to get shot of it for ever!'

'You said yourself it was a marvellous historical old place. You didn't like it either, when Maître Gérard said it would be left to fall down. And it was *her home*, her family's home back hundreds of years. Maybe she wanted to live there, to save it. After all, she's the only one left who could.'

'How can she save it, for God's sake, Roger? She's only a child!'

'She won't be a child for ever,' said Roger's mother unexpectedly from the back seat. 'If she's there, that Gérard man can't sell it from under her. He'll have to consider her wishes. If she had some help, she might be able to restore it, or — '

'The pair of you are swanning off into some cloud-cuckooland!' shouted Roger's father. 'She hasn't any money! Even when her father, a grown man, was around, they couldn't save it!'

'Her father didn't care,' said Roger's mother. 'He was hopeless, you could see. He couldn't have done anything that needed any enterprise, any will power. But Melusine — '

'Her uncle has the money,' interrupted Roger, getting more and more excited. 'She told me. If he's feeling guilty about her, maybe he'll feel guilty about the family home being sold or left to fall down. He'd be *well* ashamed if he knew she was struggling away all by herself. Maybe he'd help.'

Roger's father gaped at him.

'And you seriously think that all this was in Melusine's mind as she was driving away from the place, that she was so desperate to get back that she'd run off, *leaving you and your mother unconscious?*'

This gave Roger pause. He had thought of everything, it seemed, but this. It hurt him to think of it. At the same time he knew that Melusine might easily do just that. She'd see her chance, she'd follow her instincts. She'd do what she had to do. She would flee, like a little wild animal from a trap. Later, perhaps, she would think, and wonder, and be sorry.

'You don't understand her,' Roger said again.

'And what makes you so sure you do?'

Roger said, 'I feel it. That's all.'

There was a silence. His father, baffled and annoyed, gave a harsh, sharp sigh and rubbed his hand over his face. Then his mother said, 'Look, Brian, we're nearly there now. What's the harm in just looking? It'll put his mind at rest.'

Without a word, Roger's father let in the clutch.

The chateau stood there in the evening sun, hiding its secrets. It looked completely abandoned. But one look was enough to prove to Roger it wasn't. He knew from something other than the pull, which was now at maximum. She was here.

The ladder had been moved. Not put away. Moved to another window. And that window was slightly open.

The minute the car stopped, he was out. He ran straight to the ladder and began to climb it. He heard his father shout, but he ignored him. In a moment he was up the ladder and had slid through the open window on the first floor of the main part of the building.

He was in one of the '*chambres vides*'. The evening sun was streaming in across the floor boards. He looked down, and saw her footprints in the dust. Bare feet . . . Somewhere along that long, lonely walk, she had worn out her shoes, or taken them off. He followed the footprints.

They went out of the room, through a half-open door. Roger followed.

The corridor was half in darkness and he couldn't follow the prints. At the top of the great flight of stairs he paused. Yes, they were clear here – down the curving steps he could just make out the small imprints, and his eyes followed them across the flags of the great front hall. They didn't turn left towards the wing that had been occupied, but right, towards the ruined tower, the vast empty ballroom. . . .

But then he saw that there were also the tracks of many feet, going back and forth across the flags, making a well-beaten path in the dust through which the silvery sheen of the stone seemed to gleam. As if she had paced the length of the hall again and again . . .

He clattered down as if she were running ahead of him and he were chasing her.

He ran down the main passage to the big door at the end,

where she had once paused, before throwing it open with a seemingly indifferent '*Voilà! Le grand salon.*' When he got there, *he* paused. The pull was very strong now. But yet he didn't burst in.

Instead he knocked.

'Melusine!' he said, too softly for her to hear, because he seemed to have forgotten how to speak. Then he remembered, and, banging on the door with a hollow, penetrating sound, he shouted: '*Melusine!*'

He heard her steps, coming from a distance – quick, running steps – and then the door opened, and there she was.

He gazed at her, speechless with relief, with happiness. He was only given a second, because then she did an incredible thing. She took two swift steps towards him and flung her arms around his neck and held him tightly. He closed his eyes and hugged her. He felt her small, painfully thin body trembling in his arms. She was here! She was all right!

After a time he opened his eyes and found himself looking past her. He lowered his arms and caught his breath in amazement.

He was looking down the length of the great ballroom. But it was no longer empty. It was furnished. Not with much. She hadn't had time or strength to bring much. But near one of the long, inset windows with their shutters folded back there were two of the throne-like chairs from the big drawing-room of the flat. There was the blue-and-red rug from the twins' room. A small marquetry table that Roger recognized held some of the beautiful books. One of them was open, as if she had been reading it. . . . Her school books were heaped on the floor. There was a crystal jug of water, a dish of blackberries and hazelnuts, and, incongruously, an open tin with a silver spoon sticking out. . . .

On the window-seat was some bedding, including, as a bedspread, one of the tapestries that had hung on the drawing-room wall.

No more squalor, thought Roger dazedly. No more grime

and gloom, no more nun's cells. The grandest room in the house, and all the beauty and luxury she could carry or drag into it to make herself feel like – like a chatelaine.

She had drawn back from him and was looking into his face. She had not had any beautiful clothes to put on, and, apart from looking thinner, shabbier and more fragile, she was the same as he remembered. Except her face. Her face was filled with a fierce determination; her eyes burned and the tears of relief and joy at seeing him didn't weaken their expression.

'*Roger!*' she said, in her old, commanding tone. '*J'ai besoin de ton aide.*'

'My help?' he said, still in a daze. 'With what?'

'*La grande table,*' she said. 'The table with the pictures. I want it will be – here.'

He stared at her for a moment. That was the help she wanted! She'd need a lot more help than that, before she was finished!

He laughed suddenly.

'You must think I'm Superman! Come on, we'll get Dad to help drag it through.'

And, still laughing, he pulled her along the corridor into the great hall, and to the huge double front doors under their dusty fanlight. Together they wrestled back the old bolts, and released the chain. It was so rusty it fell to fragments.

'Now,' said Roger exultantly. 'We'll take a door each! Pull!'

And they forced the huge front doors of Chateau Bois-Serpe open to the fresh air and the golden evening sun for the first time in perhaps a hundred years.